unwritten rules

Tessa Everly

Contents

CHAPTER 1

Thania's POV

"Do you think this color brings out my eyes?" my twin sister Shania asked, holding up a red dress.

"God, of course not," I said, gagging. "It makes you look like the villain from The Minions."

She let out a laugh. I loved my twin sister to death. She was my everything.

"Thania, why don't you come with me?" she said, holding up a black dress. "I'm sorry, I don't do parties unless they're in books," I replied.

Shania and I were sisters, but we weren't the same. She thrived in the popular crowd while I was content with the adventures in my books. Mom and Dad moved us across the country two months ago. So yeah, I've been spending the entire summer reading. My mom was a stay-at-home mom. My dad was a lawyer. He was never around.

"Please, I'll give you $40 to buy that new book you want," she said, giving me puppy eyes. "I'm still not coming, and I could get it online for half price," I said, mocking her expression. "You're no fun," she said.

I had no friends here, and a party with Shania didn't sound appealing.

"You just moved here and you're already going to a party." I looked at her from head to toe. "You know me, I'm a sucker for parties."

I got up, left her room, and went straight to mine. I closed the door, sat on my bed, and opened my laptop to check my Instagram page. Even though I didn't have many followers, more than my sister and a few others, it was okay because I followed a few celebrities. Getting bored, I closed my laptop, took out a black jersey, which I liked for its style rather than its association with football, and a pair of black shorts. Then I headed to the bathroom to take a shower.

As I showered, I sang loudly, letting the music take over. "I made it through the wilderness; somehow I made it through..."I continued singing the entire song and a couple more before I finished. Wrapping a towel around myself, I stepped out of the bathroom, startled to see my twin standing there.

"Oh my God, what are you doing here? I thought you had left already," I said, trying to catch my breath.

She was laughing as if she'd heard the funniest joke ever.

"What's so funny?" I asked, puzzled. She took out her phone and showed me a video. My mouth dropped open. She had been filming me the whole time. The video showed a shadow dancing and singing.

"Let's make a deal," she said, her tone cunning. "What do you want?" I replied warily. "If you put on one of my black sneakers, some makeup, and a ponytail, you'll be party-ready." She replied.

"And if I refuse?" I asked, still not wanting to go to her party. "I post this all over Instagram and tag you," she said, holding up her phone. "Fine," I shouted in resignation. "But I'm not changing."

"Fine with me."

She stepped out of my room and went straight to hers. I sat on my bed, waiting for her return. A minute and a half later, she came back well-dressed.

We made our way to our parents' room. We knocked on the door and entered after Mom answered.

"Hey, Mom, Thania and I are going to a party. We'll be back by 1:00, okay?" Mom looked surprised, though I wasn't sure why.

She sat up on her bed and rested her right hand on my forehead.

"What's the problem?" I asked. "Are you running a fever?" she said, laughing.

Shania and I both laughed and left. I didn't bother to ask about Dad; he was either working late or out with his friends.

Our parents had bought us one car to share, and it was never a problem. About 37 minutes later, we arrived at a house with cars parked all over the driveway and kids everywhere. It was just about 9:00, and the house was almost full. I held onto Shania as she made her way to the kitchen.

"Beer?" she asked. "No, thanks," I said. "Be right back," she said, leaving me by myself.

"And oh, Thania, please mingle."

CHAPTER 2

I t had been about two hours since I'd arrived at this party, and I hated every minute of it. Shania dragged me here, then left, telling me to "mingle."

How was I supposed to mingle when I knew no one? I couldn't make friends as easily as she did. We've been here for two months now, and all I've managed to do is read two entire books. Shania, on the other hand, had already been invited to a party.

"I thought talking to yourself was illegal," I heard a voice say from behind me. Oh crap, I'd been talking to myself out loud again. It was a habit I couldn't shake.

"Oh, I'm sorry," I said, looking around and feeling like a lost puppy. "I don't bite. Come sit," the person said, patting the couch beside him.

I took a seat, still looking around. The guy started to laugh. "Why are you laughing?" I asked. "Nothing. I'm Kataon, by the way," he said, waiting for my name. "I'm Thania," I replied.

He got up from the couch and left. I had no idea why, but I didn't stress over it. As I sat there listening to the music and watching a girl throw up, Kataon returned with two cups and handed one to me.

"So, what's your story?" he asked. I gave him a puzzled look, which he noticed immediately. "Your story, as in why you're here. I know you were forced," he implied. "Oh," I said. "Well, I have a twin sister named..."

I was about to finish my sentence when a drunken Shania stumbled over and unfortunately puked all over my new boots. I stood up, trying to hold her up. "I'm sorry, I have to go," I said. "It's okay, I understand," Kataon said, gesturing toward Shania.

I tried to carry her but failed miserably. Realizing I was no good at it, Kataon got up and helped me. I pointed him toward the car.

He helped put her in, and I buckled her up before closing the door. I turned around to see Kataon staring at me. "What?" I asked. "Nothing," he said defensively. "I just wanted to say thanks for helping me with my sister and for keeping me company." I said embarrassingly. "No problem," he said, shrugging. "Here," he added, taking my phone from my hand. "Don't be afraid to use it," he said, handing it back with his number saved. "Just about now," he said, his phone vibrating. He took it out, smiled, and said, "I guess I'm more than a good boy." I smiled and shook my head.

I waved goodbye, got in the car, and drove off with Shania fast asleep. We reached home just before midnight. I woke Shania up and took her straight to her room. She fell asleep as soon as she hit the bed. I made my way to my room, changed into my pyjamas, and was about to fall asleep when my phone vibrated.

Sweet dreams. Dream about me. —Kataon

I smiled at the message and let sleep take over.

I turned over, pulled the sheets off me, and made my way to the bathroom.

After a good 15-minute shower, I got out, threw on some simple clothes, and got back on my bed. I checked my Instagram page and saw four new followers and some likes. I closed it and checked my phone. I had several new messages.

Hey. How was dreaming about me? —Kataon

Remember we have to go shopping for the first day of school. —Twin sister

How's your sister? —Kataon

I read a few more messages from Shania and Dad.

I got up and walked to my parents' room. I knocked on the door and went in. I sat on my mom's bed, but she was nowhere in sight. I scanned the room, but it didn't satisfy me, so I left. Making my way downstairs, I was greeted by a miserable twin and a hungry mom.

"Hey, what's up?" I said, jumping on the counter. "Get down; we're leaving by one," Shania said, making her way to the fridge. "Nothing's up, and get down, young miss," Mom said, slapping my leg, making me jump off the counter.

Shania buried her face in a bag of chips. I suddenly felt sad. Mom noticed and spoke up.

"What's wrong, sweetheart?" she asked. "I don't know. It's just that I haven't seen Dad much since we moved here, and I hate it," I said. "I know, darling, but it'll change," Mom answered, hugging me after noticing a tear or two falling from my eye.

CHAPTER 3

Here I was, sitting in the kitchen with Shania and Mom. The only thing missing was Dad. I paid it no mind, not wanting to cry.

"So, how was the party?" Mom asked. "It was..." Shania hesitated, not wanting to let Mom know she got drunk, as she knew she'd be grounded. "It was great," I said, holding Shania's hand.

As I was about to speak again, my phone vibrated.

Ignoring me so early? —Kataon

I smiled and asked to be excused. "Can I go to my room? Shania, text me when you're ready." I replied to the text as I made my way back to my room.

Hey, I was busy. Sorry. —Me

I finally reached my room and sat on my bed.

That's okay. I was at football practice anyway. How are you, by the way? —Kataon

I'm okay, and that's where all the muscles come from. Football. I'm good, though. How about you? —Me

All of that, huh? I know you were looking at me last night. I'm great now that I'm texting you. —Kataon

So how's your day? Can I see you today? —Kataon

My day's okay so far. I don't know, maybe. I'm going to the mall at 1:00 with my twin. —Me

I didn't realize how late it was until I heard a knock at the door. I looked up to see Shania poking her head inside. "It's time to go," she said. I got up, put on my boots, and closed my door. I kissed Mom goodbye, and Shania and I made our way to the car.

Just about to leave. Driving out right now. —Me

Be there in fifteen. —Kataon

Shania stared at me like I was some mad person.

"What?" I said. "Nothing. It's just... Okay, what's up with you? You've been smiling at your phone since we got in the car." I smiled even more. "Thania, what's up with you?" she asked, still giving me that look. Not wanting to answer, I turned on the radio and sang along to "Starboy" by The Weeknd.

About ten minutes later, we arrived at the mall. It was pretty full, mostly with teens. After finally finding a parking spot, we got out.

Didn't know your smile was this cute. —Kataon

I turned around to see a tall, blond guy smiling at me. I had to admit, he was cuter than last night. As he stepped towards us, I could see his beautiful grey eyes. He came to a standstill and started to smile, his dimples showing.

"So, uhmm," he said, rubbing the back of his neck. "I have no idea who you are, so if you know one of us, it's gotta be her," Shania said, pointing at me. "The drunk one," he said, looking at Shania. "So then, you must be Thania," he said, hugging me, and I hugged him back, of course.

Shania was staring at me. "What?" I asked. "Nothing... It's just that I've never seen you smile with a guy and actually mean it." She was smiling and shaking her head. "You've even thrown in a hug. Wait till I tell Mom."

I started laughing. Kataon was just standing there, looking back and forth. "What?" Shania said, looking at Kataon. "How do I know who's my girl?" he asked. "Your girl?" we both said in unison, causing Kataon to look a little freaked out. "You know what I mean," he said. "When you see your 'girl,' you'll know," I said to him, air-quoting the word "girl."

"Can I please ask why I'm walking around a mall with two girls who look exactly alike, which is kind of freaky, and not doing anything?" he said behind us. Shania made her way to a shoe store. Unfortunately, before we left, Mom broke the news that we should only buy shoes because we're going to a school that wears uniforms. What a bummer. "Wahoo, I like these," Shania said, walking into the third store at the mall. She bought them, paid, and left.

"Why is she only buying shoes?" Kataon asked. I explained the situation to him, and then suddenly, I felt a pull on my hand. Shania saw and followed. Kataon was leading me to God knows where. Finally, we arrived at a shoe store that looked like heaven. Shania was staring as if she was looking at a pile of gold.

I made my way over to a pair of shoes, and my eyes couldn't stop looking at the price. "Kataon, I can't afford any of these, let alone two," I said to him. "Baby doll, just relax and have a seat, please," he said, pointing to a chair. He disappeared for about a minute and came back.

"What size do you wear?" he asked. "Six and a half. Why?" I replied.

Before answering, he disappeared again.

Shania came over to where I was. "Lend me eighty dollars?" she asked. "Please." She pleads. "Why? You have three new boots already, and I don't have any yet. Why should I give you my money?" I said, looking at her puzzled. "Please, please, please," she begged. "Fine," I said, handing her the hundred-dollar bill, and immediately after, she left.

"Try these on," Kataon said, coming back with about eight pairs of shoes. "I said I can't afford any of these," I said to him.

"Baby doll," he said, giving me a look. "Fine," I said.

About five minutes later, I had tried on almost the entire section of size six and a half.

"So, which do you like?" he asked. "All of them," I said in amazement.

After another twenty minutes of picking and choosing, I finally decided on the five pairs I liked. Without a word, he left again.

CHAPTER 4

This was unusual. Where had Shania disappeared to?

"Baby doll," Kataon called, holding up two pink bags. What was he up to? "I can't," I said, gesturing that I wasn't going to take anything from him. "It's not an option," he said, shoving the bags towards me. "How can I take these from you? One pair is worth over $200." I almost shouted. "But right now, you only owe fifty-something dollars," he replied, still trying to give me the bags. "I can't," I insisted. "Look, I didn't pay for them. The store belongs to my aunt, so you get a special discount." He justified.

After about an hour of arguing, he finally won.

"Let's go get something to eat," he said, rubbing his chest. I could see all his biceps and everything. I held myself back from doing anything stupid. Behave yourself, Thania, I told myself.

"Why should you behave?" Kataon asked, clueless. Oh God. I was talking to myself again.

"Oh crap," I muttered. "Shania." I quickly made a U-turn towards where I had come from. After a minute of searching, I finally found her. Oh my God. She was all smiles with some guy.

I made my way over to her, with Kataon behind me. Still chatting away, she had no idea I was there. I cleared my throat. She looked up, startled, and so did the guy she was with. He kept looking between Shania and me.

"Hey, Travis," Kataon said, and they did that bro hug thing. "Uhmm, Travis," Shania said, glancing at me. "This is my twin sister, Thania."

"It's nice to meet you," I said, extending a hand to greet him. "I'm sorry, but we have to go."

"So, uhmm, Travis, why don't you give Shania your number so you guys can keep in touch?" I suggested. "Okay then," he said, handing his phone to Shania.

After that, they said their goodbyes, and we made our way to the exit. "You're driving," Shania said.

Upon reaching the parking lot, Kataon finally spoke. "So, this is it."

"Knowing you, I don't think so," I said, giving him a little smile. Shania was in the car, so she wasn't there to tease me. "Thania, Mom's calling," Shania said, poking her head through the car window. "I have to go," I said, about to open the door when he stopped me.

"Here," he handed me a bag. "And 'no' is not an answer." I finally gave in and took the bag. I hugged him, opened the car door, and drove off.

He was my first friend since I'd been here. Would I see him again? I wanted to, and the worst part was I didn't know why.

It was the first day of school, and I really didn't want to be late. I got up just around 6:30, just in time to catch Dad. We had a genuine conversation, and it felt like I hadn't seen him in a year. Being his little baby as always, I made us breakfast before he left.

Four pancakes later, I saw Shania making her way downstairs.

"Did you see Dad?" she asked. "Yeah," I answered. I saw sadness in her face. "He said he'll be home Saturday and Sunday," I said to her, after which I saw a little hope in her eyes.

Feeling my phone vibrate, I opened my messages.

How's my baby doll? —Kataon

She's doing just fine, and good morning to you too. —Me

Good morning. I can't wait to see you today. —Kataon

How are you gonna see me today? —Me

Don't worry, I have my ways, baby doll. —Kataon

Kataon... —Me

After my last text, there was no answer. I made my way upstairs to my room. Closing the door behind me, I saw Mom coming out of her room.

I opened my closet and took out my uniform, which was neatly pressed. I took a look at the shoes Kataon got me. I stooped down and picked up the bag. I had no idea how they looked. I took out the first pair I saw. It was a gold wedge with straps. It was beautiful.

About 45 minutes later, I was sitting downstairs, waiting on Shania.

"Please make friends, darling," my mom said in a tone as if she was begging. "I'll try," I said to her.

As she was about to answer, Shania came downstairs. We both kissed Mom goodbye and left. "I'm not driving," I heard Shania say. Why does she always do this to me?

Can't wait. —Kataon

Wait for what? —Me

Baby doll, you'll know. —Kataon

What was Kataon talking about? I thought to myself.

"What was who?" I heard Shania ask as I made my way out of the driveway. Crap. I was talking to myself out loud again.

CHAPTER 5

Nervousness gripped me as I walked through the unfamiliar corridors of the school. Everyone seemed to blend together in their uniforms, and I couldn't shake my distaste for private schools and their strict dress codes.

After locating my locker, I found a seat at the back of my first class. With the teacher yet to arrive, I plugged in my earphones, hoping to keep to myself.

You're wearing the gold one. I like it, it fits perfectly. —Kataon

I glanced around but didn't spot anyone familiar. How did Kataon know what I was wearing?

I have no idea what you're talking about.—Me

Liar. —Kataon

Before I could reply, my phone buzzed again, this time with a picture message from Kataon—of me.

Lie much? —Kataon

Where are you? —Me

No time to see if he replied, as our teacher finally entered the room.

"Good morning, class," Mrs. Donald greeted, settling at her desk. "I'm Mrs. Donald, your homeroom teacher and for those taking Spanish, your instructor."

Great, I thought sarcastically. Spanish too.

"Now, let's get started," she continued, pulling me from my thoughts. We spent the class introducing ourselves, a task I disliked immensely as the new girl in a private school.

The bell rang, signalling time for English class. I retrieved my books from my locker and headed to the next room. On my way, someone mistook me for Shania—again. It was some boy asking about history class, a subject I detested even more than being mistaken for my sister. I politely corrected him and quickly moved on.

My next class was Physics, shared with Shania. This time, I took a seat near the front, noting that the back was already full. As I settled in, a blonde girl confronted me.

"Um, you're in my seat," she declared, pointing. Not wanting any drama, I moved and found another spot, saving a seat beside me for Shania. She returned the favor by saving me a seat in Physics, which I found with relief.

Shania's POV

I practically raced to Physics class, knowing I'd be late. On the way, I was mistaken for Thania—again. It grated on me. Arriving, I quickly found a seat near the front.

Not seeing Thania, I continued scanning the room until a girl stood in front of me.

"Are you deaf? I said that's my seat," she snapped. Confused, I looked around until Thania waved me over. I grabbed my bag and moved, catching the girl muttering to herself as I left. Reuniting with Thania, we hugged and settled in. She tapped my shoulder, pointing behind me. Travis.

My excitement bubbled up. Travis was here at our school too? Why hadn't he mentioned it during our texts?

My thoughts scattered as the teacher, Mr. Brian, entered with enthusiasm.

"Good morning, young scientists," he greeted. "Let's start with introductions. I'm Mr. Brian, and I'll be your teacher this semester."

Thania seemed absorbed in her phone, so I didn't disturb her. Who was she texting?

A vibration in my pocket caught my attention. Travis.

Thania's POV

Physics class turned out to be surprisingly enjoyable, especially with Shania there too. Mr. Brian's enthusiasm made the subject engaging, though he initially mistook me for Shania, eliciting laughter from the class.

After a lively session, it was finally lunchtime. Shania and I headed to the cafeteria together. Grabbing my lunch, I received a text from Kataon.

I had no idea you were a pizza girl. —Kataon

How do you know that? And yes, pineapple, to be exact. —Me

"Who's that?" Shania asked, stealing a slice of my pizza. "It's nobody," I said quickly.

"Thania, I know you. It's never nobody when you smile like that," she teased. Before I could respond, Travis and his friends approached our table. Shania's face lit up as Travis greeted us.

"Thania or Shania?" he asked, pointing at me. "Thania," I replied, watching him direct a smile towards Shania.

He bent down to hug her, and soon they all settled around our table, some even sitting atop it.

"So, Shania, how's your day been at our school so far?" one of Travis's friends, a tall brunette named Luke, asked.

Before I could answer, my phone vibrated again.

It's been better than expected. And I'm Thania I answered Luke.

I see you've made some new friends. —Kataon

Yeah, they're quite a handful. —Me

Kataon and I continued chatting throughout lunch, while 'The Boys', as I dubbed them (since there were no girls among them), bombarded us with questions.

The school day eventually drew to a close before I knew it.

CHAPTER 6

Two days into school and Kataon seemed to know more about my day than I did. Did he attend this school too? How else would he know my class schedule and what I wore? Yesterday, he even knew what I had for lunch.

"You look a little lost." —Kataon

"No, I'm not. I just don't know anyone in the classroom." —Me

"Don't worry; you'll make a friend soon." —Kataon

Before I could respond to Kataon, one of the guys who often sat with Travis at lunch approached me.

"Thania or Shania?" he asked. "Thania," I answered. "Okay, so what's up?" he asked. "I'm Blake Collins."

"Nothing much, just feeling a bit clueless since I don't know anyone in class," I said, scanning the room. "So, are you a lot like your sister?" Blake asked. "Depends on what you want to know," I replied. "Everything," he said a hint of flirtation in his voice.

Mr Jones's timely arrival saved me from answering, as he entered the room. Calculus was one of my favourite subjects, and I eagerly awaited the lesson.

By lunchtime, I was bored to tears.

Hurry up. I'm at lunch already and we need to talk. —Twin Sister

What was up with Shania? We hadn't spoken since she nearly left me at home this morning.

After getting my lunch, I took my usual seat at our table, but 'The Boys' were nowhere to be seen. "So, what's so important it couldn't wait?" I asked Shania, munching on a piece of my pizza. She stared at me, wide-eyed, as if she wanted to scream but couldn't.

"Travis just asked me out on a date!" she exclaimed, practically shouting in my ear. "Oh my God," I replied. "When and where?"

"Yesterday at lunch, after everyone left," she replied. "Yesterday? And you didn't tell me?" I said, playfully hitting her arm. "Ouch," she winced, rubbing where I'd hit her.

Our table was soon crowded as Travis and his friends joined us, talking animatedly about football and other topics. I didn't bother to join in; instead, I just sat and listened, feeling like an outsider.

Feeling like an outsider. —Kataon

Yeah, I guess. —Me

Don't worry, one day you'll fit in just fine. —Kataon

Oh really? When? —Me

The cheerleading team. Try-outs are tomorrow. —Kataon

Me? A cheerleader? Never going to happen. —Me

I know you can do it. That body is built for cheering or danc-ing. —Kataon

Before I could respond, the bell rang, signalling the end of lunch. By the time I glanced at my phone to text Kataon back, he'd already messaged me.

Class time, huh? I'll text you after school. Later, baby doll. —Kataon

How did he know so much?

"Hey, guys, I gotta go," I announced to the table and left.

On my way to my locker, I noticed the sign-up sheet for cheerleading try-outs tomorrow.

Was Kataon right? Would I fit in there? I'd cheered at my old school, but I'd sworn I'd never cheer again. Just the thought of signing up gave me the jitters. I quickly scribbled my name on the sheet and left.

I made it to class on time and settled into a seat in the middle of the room.

"So, you wanna be a cheerleader, huh?" a tall brunette beside me asked. "Yeah, I guess," I replied. "I'm Hanna Spence," she introduced herself, offering her hand. "I'm Thania," I replied, shaking her hand. "Trust me, I know who you are."

I took a seat beside me.

She looks friendly. —Kataon

Where are you? —Me

Doll face, I'm everywhere. —Kataon

He was everywhere, clearly knowing everything without revealing how.

I hated it.

"Dinner's ready!" Mom called from downstairs. "Hurry your butts up. We have a guest!" she added.

I left my computer and headed to Shania's room, but she wasn't there. Maybe she was already downstairs.

As I descended for dinner, I heard chatter, confirming we had company.

Stepping into the kitchen, I froze.

"What's Kataon doing here?" I blurted out, causing Mom to eye me disapprovingly.

"Thania, be nice," Mom chided. "I just came by to ask how your new school is," Kataon replied, smirking.

Mom had left the kitchen briefly and returned.

"So, uh, I'm Kataon Miller," he introduced himself. "Miller?, as in Mr Miller's son, the lawyer?" Mom inquired.

"Yes, that would be me," he confirmed.

"My husband works at your dad's law firm," Mom mentioned.

Great, so his dad was my dad's boss. Just great.

"Great. I was just wondering if you'd like to stay for dinner." Mom offered. "Mom, I think Kataon is kind of busy and was just leaving," I interjected. "I would love to," Kataon accepted. This was shaping up to be the worst dinner ever, I could tell.

Shania's POV

Watching Kataon, Thania, and Mom in the kitchen was like watching a soap opera.

Kataon was nice enough, and he managed to make Thania smile, but something was off. She looked pissed, and I could tell.

"So, Kataon, do you go to school?" I asked, trying to ease the tension.

Thania looked intrigued by my question. "I go to a private school," Kataon answered. "So, Thania," he turned to her, changing the subject. "See any extracurricular activities at school you like?" "Yeah, I'm trying out for the cheerleading team," Thania announced.

"What?" I exclaimed.

Thania, trying out for the cheer team? When did that happen?

Back home, Thania was co-captain and I was captain of our cheer team, leading us to three championships. We'd sworn we'd never cheer again.

I didn't say a word; I just turned and ran straight to my room.

How could she do that?

CHAPTER 7

Thania's POV

I hadn't expected Kataon to show up at my house. How did he even know where I lived in the first place?

As I prepared to leave the table, Kataon's phone rang. He excused himself and stepped away.

A few moments later, he returned.

"Sorry, but I have to go," I heard him say to my mom. "That's okay, sweetheart. Come back anytime," my mom replied warmly.

I escorted him to the door, but we walked in silence. I watched as he drove off, closed the door behind me, and headed upstairs.

I knew Shania was upset with me, but I hated it when we weren't on good terms. Pushing open her door, I peeked inside and then walked in, taking a seat on her bed.

"Look, Shania, I'm sorry, okay? It's just that everyone at school warms up to you instantly. No one ever mistakes me for Thania; they always ask if I'm Shania, and I hate it. I thought maybe trying out for the cheer team would help me fit in," I explained.

"Do you think it's easy for me to fit in? No, it's not. I constantly get mistaken for the 'beauty with brains' twin. I hate when people ask if I'm Thania, the brainiac who's cute. Travis is the only normal thing that's happened to me," Shania replied sharply, but I said nothing.

"If trying out for the cheer team helps you fit in, then fine, I'll try out with you. But if only one of us makes it, then neither of us will," she declared. "Wait, so does that mean you're trying out with me too?" I asked eagerly.

"Well, maybe," she replied, giving me a sidelong glance. We hugged it out, and I left her room feeling a bit relieved.

Later, when I returned to the dining room, Kataon was gone, and Mom was clearing the table.

Sorry about tonight. I just wanted to see you, and I had no idea what was going to happen. —Kataon

I didn't bother replying; instead, I went straight back to my computer to check my Instagram.

Answer me, please. —Kataon

Still, I didn't respond.

If you don't answer me, I'll be coming for dinner tomorrow night. —Kataon

What do you want, Kataon? —Me

I'm sorry.—Kataon

I know you are. —Me

I was so exhausted that I didn't notice if Kataon had texted me back. I just let sleep take over.

Kataon's POV

I couldn't wait to go back to school on Monday. Texting her every day and not seeing her—I had to do something.

She had no idea that she was coming to my school. Travis and the guys kept telling me more about her every day. They sent me pictures when I asked and told me everything I wanted to know.

I'd texted her couple of minutes ago, and since she didn't reply, I knew she'd fallen asleep.

I sent her one last text for the night.

Good night, doll face. Sleep tight and sweet dreams. —Me

I heard my mom yelling from downstairs, so I got up and made my way down.

"Hey, Mom, were you calling?" I asked. "Yes, I was. I've been calling you for about a minute now. Where are your manners, young man?" she scolded me. "I'm sorry, Mother. May I ask why you were yelling like you're insane?" I teased.

She swatted my arm lightly. "I was just calling to tell you that there'll be company on Saturday night. Your dad's throwing a business party, and a few business partners will be coming over," she explained in a stern tone.

I smiled, kissed her cheek, and left.

My dad's business dinners were always dull affairs, filled with old men asking about football and playing dreadful music.

Oh God, it was going to be boring.

Shania's POV

Finally, it was Friday, and I was relieved. Today, Thania drove us to school; I said nothing as I got out of the car. Thania and I hadn't had a decent conversation since that dinner with Kataon.

I headed to my locker, retrieved my books, and closed it when Travis startled me.

"So, how about our date tomorrow?" he asked, a hopeful look in his eyes.

I'd completely forgotten about Travis and me. We had a date tomorrow night.

"I'm sorry, I can't," I replied sadly. "Oh," he said quietly. "I was looking forward to our date."

"I know, I'm sorry. It's just that my dad is having this dinner party, and my mom, Thania, and I are going," I explained.

He looked crestfallen.

As he turned to leave, I spoke up. "You could come, and we'll call it a date," I suggested.

He turned back, a smile spreading across his face. I quickly scribbled the address on a piece of paper, handed it to him, smiled, and headed off to class.

I had a date tomorrow. Oh my God.

I needed major help, so I texted Thania our secret code for "SOS. I have a date. Help."

SOS. Travis. —Me

Oh my God. I have the perfect dress for you. Anyways, gotta go. I have History. —Twin Sister

Okay, thanks. I love you. —Me

I couldn't believe it—I had a date with Travis. I smiled to myself and made my way to class.

Thania's POV

The bell rang, signaling the end of lunch. I stood up and headed outside. On my way to my locker, my phone vibrated. It was Kataon, but I ignored it. I made my way to class and found a seat at the front.

Great, we'd only been in school for less than a week, and Shania already had a date.

"Can you explain number 3 to us, Miss Harris?" Mr. Martin asked me in History class.

He snapped me out of my thoughts, but I was clueless.

"Number 3, Miss Harris?"

"Oh... Uh... World War Three began on July 28, 1914, and lasted until November 11, 1918. The war began because on June 28, 1914, Archduke Franz Ferdinand, the heir to the Austrian throne, was visiting the town of Sarajevo, Bosnia, when he was shot by a Serbian student," I answered nervously.

"Wonderful. At least someone is paying attention."

As he started to explain further, the bell rang for our next class. "Test next week, Friday, people", he reminded us before dismissing us.

CHAPTER 8

Thania's POV

Finally, it was lunchtime.

Reflecting on my history class earlier, I checked my messages from Kataon.

Hey doll face. —Kataon

Ignoring me now. —Kataon

I know you were thinking about me in history class. —Kataon

I still couldn't figure out how Kataon knew so much about my school. Grabbing my lunch, I sat down at our usual table with one of the boys out of the five.

"Hey, I'm Hayden," he greeted, waving at me. "Hi," I replied. "Thania or Shania?" he inquired. "Thania," I confirmed.

Just as Hayden was about to respond, a petite blonde approached and kissed him on the cheek. He turned, realizing who it was, and returned the kiss. Startled, she turned and noticed me there, then looked back at Hayden.

"Oh, um, Thania, this is my girlfriend, Joanna Anderson," he introduced. Joanna waved at me, and I returned the gesture.

I heard some noise and looked up to see the rest of the group approaching.

My phone vibrated, and I knew it was Kataon.

Was he flirting? —Kataon

No, that's his girlfriend. And what if he was? —Me

Oh, I thought he was. I would kill him. —Kataon

How do you know where I am or who I'm with or all those things? —Me

I have my perks. By the way, tell Shania I said hi. —Kataon

That still doesn't answer my question. And okay, I will. —Me

Gotta go, doll face. Talk to you later. And if he flirts, I'll know. —Kataon

I smiled at his last message, realizing I hadn't touched my lunch. I took a bite of my pizza, not wanting to break the conversation, and texted Shania.

Kataon says hi.—Me

She glanced at the message, smiled, and nodded.

Finally, lunch was over, and I was exhausted from hearing about football.

See you in tryouts.—Twin Sister

Okay, see you. —Me

I couldn't believe Shania was actually going to try out just for me. I couldn't wait for tryouts.

Next up was calculus. I wondered how someone with a brain could fail calculus. Arriving at class, I took a seat, hearing a lot of chatter around me, but I didn't bother to join in.

"Hey, Thania, right?" someone said. I looked up to see Joanna, Hayden's girlfriend. "Yes," I replied, relieved that someone here actually got my name right. "I'm Hayden's girlfriend," she introduced herself. "Yeah, I remember. Joanna, right?" I confirmed.

Before she could answer, a group of girls entered, talking about tryouts happening today.

"That's Kamera," Joanna pointed to the blonde-haired girl. "She's the head cheerleader. And those two, Brooke and Stephanie, are her minions," she added, clearly indicating two other girls.

I tried to place where I'd seen Joanna before.

"She sits in the middle front row in every class," Joanna finished. And suddenly, it all clicked. She was the blonde I accidentally sat in the seat of on Monday during homeroom.

Hey baby doll. I've been busy trying on tuxes. See you after school. The mall? —Kataon

I would give anything to see you in a tux. I have tryouts. Are you willing to wait? —Me

So, what about your sister? Is she trying out too? —Kataon

"Thania?" Johanna said pulling my attention from my phone.

"Oh, sorry. You were saying?" I replied. "Your sister, is she trying out also?" Johanna clarified.

"Yeah, she is, but only because of me," I replied. "Okay, cool," Johanna said before walking back to her seat behind me.

Dinner at my house tomorrow night? Wear something sexy. It's a formal event. —Kataon

As much as I'd love to, I have plans with my family. —Me

I didn't know if Kataon had replied because the teacher entered the classroom, prompting me to quickly shove my phone into my bag before he noticed.

"Guess what?" Mr. Smith announced, holding up some papers. "Pop quiz," he declared. The entire class groaned, and so did I. I hated days like these.

About half an hour later, I finally left the classroom, scanning the area for Shania. My phone vibrated again.

Kataon. —Me

Okay then, as long as I get to take you out sometimes. —Kataon

Looking for sis. Check the field, bleachers.—Kataon

How did he know that? How?

Are you asking me out on a date? —Me

How would you know that? —Me

Baby doll, how many times do I have to tell you I have my ways? I gotta go, see you later, and good luck in tryouts. —Kataon

Following Kataon's instruction, I made my way to the field and looked where he had directed me.

My jaw dropped.

Travis.

Shania.

Oh my God.

After about ten seconds of standing there in shock, Shania finally noticed me and looked surprised. But after a moment, she began smiling like she was crazy.

"See you in tryouts," Travis said, kissing her on the forehead.

"Thania," he greeted me. "Travis," was all I managed to reply.

The cheers echoing through the gym made me second-guess myself. But seeing how nervous I looked, Shania came over and held my hand. It was strangely comforting. Suddenly, the noise died down, and I looked up to see the three "minions": Brooke, Stephanie, and Kamera.

"Thania," someone called, not to me but to Shania.

She pointed at me.

"Hey," the girl greeted me. "Hanna," I said, somewhat surprised. "Yeah, I didn't know you'd remember me," she remarked. "Well, I do."

After what felt like an hour, tryouts finally ended. Exhausted, I pleaded with Shania to drive since I was always the one driving.

Once home, I peeled off my uniform and threw it in the laundry, then headed to the bathroom. After a good half-hour, I wandered into the kitchen to find Mom there.

"How were tryouts?" she asked. "They were great," I replied. "A bit tiring, though."

"I got a job," she blurted out suddenly.

I started to smile. "That's great," I said enthusiastically.

"Well, it's not really a job," she clarified.

Looking up, I saw Shania coming down the stairs.

Mom explained that it was a shop she wanted to turn into a pastry shop, where she could sell flowers and set up tables and chairs for customers.

"So, what do you guys think?" Mom asked eagerly. "I've already talked to your dad, and he's okay with it. I hate being home all day with nothing to do at times, it's annoying. I want to go back to work, you know?"

"I'm great with it, and I'd be glad to help," I offered, making my way upstairs with a bag of chips.

As I settled on my bed, I suddenly heard either Mom or Shania closing my bedroom door.

CHAPTER 9

Thania's POV

Turning in my bed, I felt my phone vibrating for about the tenth time. I was going to ignore it when it vibrated again. Dragging myself to the bathroom, I spotted the soda I'd left there beside a bag of chips. I reached for the soda and found it warm, remembering that I had left it out. Then it hit me.

Kataon.

I was supposed to meet him at the mall. How long had I been asleep? Checking my phone, I saw five messages from Kataon.

Still on for the mall? —Kataon

I'm here, where are you? —Kataon

Are you still coming? Because I'm still here waiting. —Kataon

You know, you're the first girl to ever stand me up. —Kataon

If you're not going to answer, I'm coming over. —Kataon

Oh my God, Kataon must hate me for not showing up. And then, my mind went back to the last message. He was coming over.

That was sent 15 minutes ago. Oh my God, he was coming over.

Startling me, rocks began hitting my window. I opened it and looked down.

Kataon.

Oh my God. He wasn't joking.

I want to talk to you. Waiting in my car. —Kataon

A million thoughts ran through my head. Should I go or not?

Well, maybe I should.

I didn't bother to change, just grabbed my hoodie and quietly made my way outside. I ran across to his car and slid into the passenger seat. Taking off my hoodie, Kataon spoke.

"You stood me up?"

I knew this was coming.

"No, I didn't. I'm so sorry about today," I said, feeling sad. "So?" he replied.

"So what?"

"Why didn't you show?"

I turned towards him and explained why I couldn't make it to the mall. The car was silent for about a minute and a half before Kataon started the engine and drove off.

Where was he going?

The car finally came to a stop about six minutes later. Kataon didn't leave the car, so I stayed put.

Grabbing the steering wheel, I noticed his knuckles were covered in blood, as if he had hit a hard surface like a wall.

I placed my hand on his, and he looked up at me, showing every emotion he was feeling. What had happened?

"What happened here?" I asked, not expecting a reply. He finally spoke. "The wall happened."

"What did you do? Did you hit it or something?"

He said nothing. Looking into his eyes, I spoke again.

"Why are you doing this to yourself?"

He still said nothing but gently intertwined our hands. As if the universe felt my pain and sadness, it began to rain. Stuttering, he finally spoke.

"May I have this dance?"

I didn't reply. I rested my other hand on the glass window, feeling the cold. Turning towards me, he spoke again.

"Shall we?"

Not wanting to say no, I answered.

"We shall."

Opening the door silently, I was startled by a grinning twin.

"Oh my God, don't ever do that again. Why are you laughing so much?" I asked her. "Mom came in to look for you," she replied.

The look on my face gave me away; I was dead grounded.

Thania started to laugh again. "Don't worry, I covered for you."

A sigh of relief escaped me. "So, spill. And why are you wet?"

"We danced in the rain."

"You danced... in the rain?" she asked in a surprise. "Yes, Shania. Now stop looking at me like that."

I made my way to the bathroom and slipped under the warm water. It felt so good. After my shower, Shania still hadn't left. Drying my hair, I saw my phone light up.

It was a message from Kataon.

Grabbing my phone, Shania was smiling like an idiot.

"Can I have my phone back, please?" Trying to grab my phone from Shania, I finally gave up, and she handed it back to me.

Sweet dreams. Remember to dream about me. —Kataon

Smiling like an idiot, Shania began to laugh, but I didn't mind. "Don't you plan on leaving?" I asked showing her the door.

"Nope. Speaking of leaving, Dad's here, and he said to tell you that we'd be going to a dinner tomorrow night at one of his business partners' houses."

"Dad's here and you're just telling me that? And I already know about the dinner."

"He's tired, okay." After Shania spoke, the room went silent.

Climbing up on my bed, Shania gave me a look she hadn't in years. "Yes, you can sleep with me tonight." I laughed at her as she squealed.

A smile crept upon her face as she lay beside me. Turning towards me, she spoke.

"I love you, Thania, and I'm glad that you're my sister."

"I love you too, Shania."

"Good morning, my loves."

The sun hit my face as I turned in bed. Waking up to a body next to mine, I remembered last night when Shania asked to sleep beside me.

"My little Strawberry and my little Blueberry, wake up."

Strawberry? There was only one person who called me that, and it was Dad. Opening my eyes, I saw my dad sitting on the edge of my bed.

"Daddy!"

"Yes, it's me, Strawberry."

I said nothing more and jumped into his arms. After about a minute, still in his arms, Shania finally woke up. I left them both and made my way to the bathroom to freshen up.

After coming out, both Dad and Shania were gone. "Hey Mom, what's for breakfast?" I asked.

"Get down off the countertop, young lady. How many times have I told you about that?" Mom said, tapping my leg.

"I'm sorry, Mom."

"Hey, sweetheart," my mom responded to my dad.

"Yes, honey?"

"Should I wear a white tuxedo or a black one tonight?" he asked. "I don't know, honey, just pick a color already."

Out of nowhere, Shania spoke up. "Oh, I have an idea, a great one at that."

"Oh, and what would that 'great idea' be?" I said, air-quoting her. "Oh, Thania, shut up. Anyways, Mom, do you remember those white dresses we had for your 7th-anniversary party but never wore again?"

"Yeah, I remember. Mine's been in my closet for three years." I chuckled.

"Yeah, we can wear them while Daddy wears his white tuxedo."

"That's a brilliant idea," Mom said. Looking clueless, my dad finally spoke, "So it's white, then, right, darling?"

"Yes, honey, white." Finally. My family was complete and happy. Finally.

CHAPTER 10

Thania's POV

"So this is it?" my dad said, looking pleased. "Remember to smile. If I get this promotion, I'll be home three days a week, all day."

Pushing the door open, all eyes were on us. We were like royalty. My dad was in a white tuxedo, with a white shirt, white shoes, and a white watch. My mom wore a white dress like Shania and me, paired with gold stilettos, a gold chain, matching earrings, and a bracelet.

Shania and I wore the same dresses as Mom, except for the shoes. I was wearing the ones Kataon gave me.

About half an hour later, Mom and Dad were on the dance floor, and so were Shania and Travis.

Wait, Travis? What was he doing here?

"May I have this dance?" I heard a voice behind me.

"No, thanks," I replied without turning around. I wasn't a great dancer and didn't want to embarrass myself.

"Really, baby doll? Nobody has ever turned me down."

Then I recognized the voice.

Kataon.

I turned around to see a smiling Kataon. "So, may we?"

"We may."

Kataon and I made our way to the dance floor, joining my mom and dad along with Travis and Shania. Fifteen minutes later, my dad introduced us to his boss, Kataon's dad, and his mom, along with a little girl, who I assumed was their daughter.

She was absolutely lovely.

"So, Mr. Harris," my dad's boss spoke. "How are your lovely ladies enjoying the party so far?"

"It's great," I said, as if speaking for the three of us.

"This is my little daughter, Faith," he said, pointing toward the little girl. "And our son is around here somewhere." He was now looking all over the room. A few minutes later, I was bored. Noticing this, Mr. Miller spoke.

"I hope you enjoy the rest of your night," he said, then gestured to my dad to follow him. I watched as they walked off into their deep conversation. Turning around, Mom was off with Mrs. Miller while Shania was with Faith. I went to find a spot where no one was and luckily, I did.

Sitting down, wishing I was at home in bed, my phone vibrated. As always, it was Kataon.

Where are you? —Kataon

I'm on the highway to hell. —Me

Laughing real hard Someone like you should be in heaven, not hell. —Kataon

Only angels are in heaven. —Me

Exactly. —Kataon

Smile —Me

You still haven't told me where you are. —Kataon

I guess you'll never know. —Me

Babydoll, I always know where you are. —Kataon

Well then, we'll just have to wait and see. —Me

I had no idea that I was smiling like an idiot until I heard someone clear their throat. I looked up to see a tall figure standing before me. I had no idea who it was.

"Is this seat taken?" he said, pointing beside me. "No, you can sit," I replied shyly.

"You have a cute smile," he said, causing me to turn red.

"I'm Kevin," he said, extending his hand. I shook it gently, and he started to smile, showing his dimples.

He told me a little about himself, and I reciprocated.

He went to an all-boys private school in a nearby town. And did I mention he was gay? What a waste. We sat down talking about random stuff like clothes, parties, and a lot more. We exchanged numbers and continued our conversation.

About a minute later, a smiling Shania approached us.

Kevin looked freaked out. "Oh, Kevin," I said, touching his arm. "This is my twin sister Shania. You can tell us apart by a lot of things. For example, she's a brunette while I have brown hair. I'm a little taller, and last but not least, I have three ear piercings while she has two."

"Uhm. Okay. Then, all I want to know is that you're Thania and she's Shania."

"Anyways, why were you smiling like an idiot?" Kevin asked Shania. "Because Travis just asked me to be his girlfriend," she said, smiling. "And who is this Travis?" Kevin asked.

After explaining to Kevin about Travis, he spoke. "Is he my type?"

All three of us started to laugh. Suddenly, we were disturbed by a tall figure standing before us in the dark.

"Hey, babe," the person said. Babe? Since when was I somebody's babe?

And suddenly, I knew that voice.

Kataon.

I let out a sigh and spoke.

"Hi, Kataon."

"Why so sad? Not happy to see me?" I didn't answer.

He came closer and waved to Shania after giving Kevin a bad look. "May I borrow my girlfriend a bit?" he said, grabbing my hand and leading me away. Here he goes again, calling me his girlfriend, but I knew he thought Kevin was hitting on me.

I waved goodbye and mouthed "later" to both Kevin and Shania, then followed Kataon.

CHAPTER 11

"You look beautiful," Kataon said, making me smile. We had left the party and were walking around. "Where are you taking me?" I asked. He said nothing.

He took my hand and led me into a dark room. I was scared but trusted Kataon. Ok, maybe I trusted him a lot. I heard the door shut behind me, which startled me.

Quietly, he spoke softly in my ear, "Close your eyes." Agreeing, I closed my eyes. A few seconds later, I felt Kataon's arms wrapped around me.

"Open your eyes," he said. Opening my eyes, I stood still.

It was beautiful.

"I know it isn't much, but I thought you might like it," Kataon said, running a hand through his hair. "You can come here anytime you want. It belongs to me." I had never seen so many books in my entire life.

"It's beautiful," I said to him. "I love it."

I walked around, rubbing my fingers against each book my fingers could touch. The ceiling had a gold chandelier hanging from it.

It was absolutely beautiful.

Turning around, I bumped into a hard chest. Looking up, I saw Kataon smiling. Removing hair from my face, he spoke.

"Be with me."

My mind went blank. Breaking the silence, I spoke. "Ok."

Letting out a chuckle, he spoke. "Kiss me." Wait, did he just ask me to kiss him?

Without further hesitation, I felt his lips pressed against mine. I did nothing but return the kiss. Oh my God, I was kissing Kataon Miller.

MONDAY MORNING. THREE WEEKS LATER

"Guys, let's go! I don't want to be late for my first day of work," Mom shouted from downstairs.

My mom opened her café on Saturday, and the opening was great, but today was the first day of official business. It was Mom's first day at her new shop, and it was on our way to school, so with one car taken by Dad for work, that left only one.

"I'm coming, give me a minute," I called. "Well, hurry up then, would you?" she replied.

Rushing downstairs, I found Shania already there. "I'm not driving," was all I could say.

Both Mom and I turned towards Shania.

"Fine, I'll drive."

"Hey, cute shoes, Thania," Mom said, causing me to blush.

After dropping Mom off at her new café, Shania and I made it to school just in time to hear the bell ring. After leaving my locker, I made my way to homeroom for our first session.

About a minute into class, Miss finally came. A blushing Shania was beside me with Travis, as if they were in their own little love bubble.

Breaking me out of my thoughts, my phone vibrated.

That is how I want you to be smiling when you see me. —Kataon

What did he mean by that?

Just as I asked myself that question, it was answered. Kataon walked through the door, causing the entire homeroom to stare at him and a few girls to squeal.

"Very nice of you to join us, Mr. Miller, one month later," said the teacher.

Kataon.

He came to this school. That explained why he always knew so much about me and why Travis was always taking pictures of me—they knew each other.

Snapping me out of my thoughts was a loud crash next to me. "Hey, babydoll."

I turned to face a smiling Kataon. I said nothing.

And the moment I had been waiting for—the bell.

Rushing out of homeroom, I hurried to Spanish class, avoiding the one person I wanted to see.

Kataon.

And I managed to avoid him for the entire day, until lunch.

At lunch, I sat at our regular table, along with everyone else and one extra person: Kataon.

I overheard Blake talking to Kataon.

"Bro, where have you been? Why didn't you show up for the first month of school? It's been boring without you, man. Coach has been pressuring us hard, and unfortunately, no captain was there."

"You know how I hate the first few weeks—so much about knowing new people, new teachers, and a whole lot of crap."

"Hey, Thania, right?" I heard an overexcited Joanna ask. "Yeah, that's me," I said.

"You guys made it!"

I had no idea what she was talking about and felt clueless.

"The cheer team—you guys made it."

"Oh. Ok. I guess."

Digging into my fruit salad, I felt my phone vibrate.

Cheer up, our kids are going to be so glad their mom was a cheerleader. —Kataon

I let out a chuckle.

Our kids. I beg to differ. Thanks, by the way. MY kids will appreciate it. —Me

I don't think so. —Kataon

We'll just have to wait and see. —Me

Ok. I will. —Kataon

I have to go, talk to you later. —Me

"Mom, I'm home!" I yelled upstairs as I stepped through the door with Shania behind me.

I walked into the kitchen to see both my parents around the table, smiling as if they'd won the lottery or something.

"Thania, my darling," my dad said, hugging me. "Where's your sister?" he asked.

I yelled for Shania to come into the kitchen.

We all took a seat around the table, with Shania and I both clueless. Looking at my mom, my dad finally spoke.

"I got that promotion!" my dad yelled.

I said nothing. I hadn't even noticed I was crying. I didn't know if it was tears of joy or something else.

I went to hug my dad and congratulated him.

"Now I'll be home for two days a week and early on others. You're looking at newest senior partner"

My mom served dinner, and we started having conversations about my dad's promotion, school, and even my mom's new job.

I looked at my twin sister, my dad, and my mom, and I started to smile.

CHAPTER 12

Thania's POV

Three weeks had gone by, and I felt pain all over from head to toe. Everywhere hurt. Cheerleading practice was intense. Shania seemed used to the pain, and don't get me wrong, I was used to it too, but now I had no idea what it felt like to not be sore.

Kataon and I hadn't had a good conversation since we went to the movies last week with Blake and Amber. He was busy with football, and I was busy with the squad. Breaking me out of my thoughts, my phone vibrated. I looked down to see Kataon's name pop up. I opened the message and read it aloud.

Meet me outside in a minute —Kataon

Ok —Me

I wanted to rest, but I wanted to see Kataon too. I sent Shania a text message telling her that I'd be out and she needed to cover for me. Dad was home, and I definitely didn't want to be grounded.

I made my way outside to see Kataon leaning against a motor-cycle.

"Hey, what's this all about?" I asked.

He didn't answer but shoved his helmet at me and gripped me by the waist, placing me on the bike. Without a word, he got on and sped off.

Five minutes later, we came to a stop. He took me off the bike and removed the helmet from my head. Finally, in what felt like forever, he spoke.

"I need you to put this on," he said, holding out a blindfold. I looked at him, then at the blindfold, then back to him.

I didn't protest. I put the blindfold on, and I felt Kataon's hands tying it at the back. After that, I felt him leading me down a path.

Kataon, where the hell are we going? I thought to myself. Or maybe I said it out loud.

"We're going somewhere, and I won't hurt you," he replied.

That's when I realized I hadn't just thought it—I'd said it out loud. I hate when that happens.

Suddenly, we came to a stop. Kataon gently took the blindfold off, and what I saw in front of me was so beautiful I thought I was going to cry.

"It... it's... beau...tiful," I managed to say with tears streaming down my face.

It was a blanket laid out with roses all over it and a candle on a stand in the middle. There was food and everything that made it look like a dinner. What made it even more perfect was that there was a lake overlooking it all.

It was beautiful.

"It was nothing I couldn't handle," I said, causing Kataon to laugh. "Yeah, you fell on your butt though," he replied, making me laugh even harder.

Ten minutes into our dinner, Kataon and I were talking about my first day ever cheering at my old school.

"Yeah, maybe two or three times," I said, causing Kataon to laugh so hard that I started laughing again. "Want to go for a swim?" he asked.

I didn't answer but looked out at the lake. I shrugged, causing Kataon to smile.

I got up and walked towards the lake, allowing my feet to touch the water. It was warm. I turned to a smiling Kataon.

"Shall we?" he asked.

I looked up and bit my lip, causing Kataon to let out a sound like a moan. I paid it no mind. I looked at the water, then at him, finally answering.

"We may."

"Okay, guys, let's start with a simple routine. I'm going to put you in groups of four, and each group gets to make a simple routine that will wow everybody," our cheer captain announced.

Cheer practice was getting easier because, for one, my body was getting used to the pressure again, and two, I could watch Kataon play football all day.

"Thania... Thania..." the captain called.

"Uh, yes?" I hadn't realized I was daydreaming again.

"You're with Alecia, your sister, and Taina," she said.

I nodded my head, walking over to my partners. I was surprised she let Shania and me be in the same group.

Rumour had it that she didn't want us on the team, but Coach said if she didn't add us, she'd no longer be captain.

I looked up to see Hanna and Joanna. I waved hello with a simple smile. They were in the same group. Just then, I noticed that Brooke was placed in a group but not Stephanee. I cleared my throat and walked up to Kamera, our so-called captain. I got everyone's attention. Looking at her supposed BFF, I spoke.

"Why isn't Stephanee in a group when there's one over there with only three people?" Kamera was silent for a moment, then she spoke. "Because I didn't place her in one."

"And why's that?" I asked. Before Kamera could answer, Stephanee spoke. "I wasn't placed in a group because I'm special, unlike you."

"How special can you be?" I asked, but this time it was Kamera who answered. "Very special," she said.

Just then, the entire football team walked in. I could hear girls whispering to each other and pointing. In the corner of my eye, I could see Joanna and Hayden. Turning around, I saw Jaiden and Hanna playing around while Travis was chatting away with Shania. I sighed.

Coming back to the real world, I felt a hard shove. Looking up, I saw Kamera making her way over to the one person I hadn't noticed yet: Kataon.

"Hey, babe," was all I heard before getting mad.

CHAPTER 13

B abe.

What the hell.

"No, Kamera. It's Kataon, not babe." I exhaled a sigh of relief.

"My place later, say about 7?" I was sure I was going to gag after I saw her wink.

"No thanks, that's never going to happen," I smiled, looking at him.

I could see Shania watching me from the corner of her eye. I didn't interfere in whatever they had going on, and I definitely didn't want anything to do with Kataon, let alone Kamera and Kataon.

"How many times have I said no, Kam? We. Are. Never. Happening." Didn't she have a little pride? "Now, to the real reason I'm here." This time he was looking at me.

"Hey, babe." I looked around to see if he was actually talking to me.

"Thania." I looked up to see Kataon standing right in front of me. I can't say I wasn't blushing.

"Yes?" was all I could manage to say. "Babe," he repeated.

This time, I didn't answer.

"Our secret place later, say around 7:30?"

At first, I had no idea what he was talking about, but then he looked at me, and I realized he meant where we were last night.

"Ok, I'll be there." I heard whispers all around the room. I could also hear Shania, Hanna, and Joanna snickering to each other. So cliché.

"Ok, I'll pick you up later. Bye, babe." He planted a kiss on my cheek and gestured to the rest of the guys. Before they went through the door, he stopped and turned back, looking at me.

"And oh, this time bring something sexy to bathe in." He blew me a kiss and left with the rest of the guys.

I was sure I was red by now. What the hell just happened? I felt eyes all over me. And I also felt a death glare, and I knew it was from Kamera.

I could sense a new enemy slowly approaching.

Slowly turning around, I saw Hanna, Joanna, and Shania grinning at me. I walked over to them and started a conversation.

About a minute later, we were interrupted by Kamera.

"Practice dismissed." I could practically hear her shouting.

This was going to be a long school year.

I had no idea what happened earlier today. I was leaning up against the car, waiting for Shania to get her tongue out of Travis's mouth and her butt in the car.

I swear to God I was going to hurl or pass out. Did I mention that I was bored?

"Hey, baby doll," I looked up to see a smiling Kataon. "So, are we still on for later?" Later. Oh, the lake.

"Yeah, we are. May I ask what that was all about?"

"What are you talking about?"

"Cheer practice. Kamera. The whole 'babe' thing."

"Oh, that." I could see the anger in his face."So?" I replied dryly. "Explain."

"Okay, look, it's like this: Kamera and I used to be a fling back in sophomore year. I ended it the summer before senior year. And she still thinks we're a thing. We never had an actual relationship. It was always sex with no strings attached."

I kept silent.

"I...I...uhm..." Was I stuttering? Use your words, Thania.

"Say something. Please."

"I don't know what to say."

I sighed. A part of me was sad, and the other half was, well, let's just say happy.

"Okay."

He grinned, maybe even smiled.

"I'll pick you up tonight at 7. Bring a swimsuit." He kissed me on the cheek, then got on his bike and drove off.

Getting into the car, I noticed Shania was there. She almost scared the living hell out of me.

"Why so surprised? You were the one hurrying us up."

"I'm not surprised, Shania. You scared me." I heard her chuckle.

"How long have you been here?"

"Long enough to know you'll be midnight skinny-dipping later."

I slapped her on the shoulder.

"Be careful, Thania. We don't want Travis going ballistic on you for hurting his girlfriend now."

I started laughing.

I just realized that we were still sitting in an empty car park.

"Whatever. Let's go home. Daddy's going to be home early today; he might even cook."

We both started to laugh.

Let's just say that the only thing my dad can cook without burning or turning into something else is mac and cheese. Before we moved here, back when Mom had a job, she would always be out, and when Dad was home first, he tried to cook.

We tried to have a family dinner one Sunday where Dad decided to cook because, according to him, Mom was stressed and needed to relax.

He tried to cook noodle casserole.

But it turned out to be something similar to soup.

Trust me, I'll never live that one down.

"Aren't you going to drive?"

"Okay, sorry. Let's get home to mac and cheese." We both had to laugh at that one.

With nothing more, I drove off thinking about tonight.

Thinking about Kataon.

CHAPTER 14

I was in my room preparing for later.

"Hey, kiddo."

I looked up to see my dad with a smile plastered on his face.

"Your mom told me you were going on a date." Way to go, Mom.

"Yeah, sorry I didn't tell you." He looked at me, a mix of pride and sadness in his eyes.

"Look, pumpkin, you're everything a dad could want. You don't party, you don't drink or smoke, you don't have tattoos or navel piercings, only piercings on your ears, which I'm totally okay with, and you wear clothes that cover your body because you choose to. I understand you've never been on a date before, but if this guy doesn't appreciate you, he's nothing but an ass."

"Thanks, Daddy. I love you."

"I love you too, Berry."

"Uh... so can we get in on that hug?" I looked up to see Mom and Shania standing at my doorway.

"Oh, what the hell."

They both came over, and now the four of us were sitting on my bed hugging. It was weird but nice.

"So, Mom, how much of that did you hear?"

"Enough." I chuckled softly.

"So, how's the shop, honey?" Only my dad has been to my mom's café since it opened, and I felt a little bad.

"Oh my god, Mom, I'm so sorry. It's just that I've been busy with practice and stuff, but I promise you I'll be there tomorrow night."

"That's okay, darling. And don't you have a date to get ready for?"

Upon saying that, they left, leaving me alone sitting on my bed, with no clue how to get ready.

After having a shower and doing all the necessary things, I decided on a dress and simple platform shoes.

Not knowing whether or not to pack something for the lake, I texted Kataon.

Still on for the lake? Thania

Dropping my phone down, I went to my mirror. I didn't put on any makeup except lip balm and put my hair up in a messy bun.

Hearing my phone ring, I grabbed it and answered, seeing it was Kataon.

"Hello." Really, Thania? Hello?

"Hey beautiful, change of plans. You're coming to meet the family. My cousin Isabelle is coming over, and we're having a dinner. I told them I have a date, but they insisted on you coming, so wear something casual but sexy and nice. Be there in 5."

He didn't even allow me to answer; he just hung up.

A million thoughts went through my head. Oh my god. I'm going to meet Kataon's parents as his girlfriend, not my dad's boss's daughter.

I searched my entire closet for something to wear until I finally found it. It was the dress I wore to my parents' anniversary barbecue party.

Exactly 4 ½ minutes later, Kataon arrived at my doorstep. He had a friendly conversation with Shania and my parents.

Upon leaving, I saw Shania in a pair of pants and my boots that she had taken an interest in, with a plain crop top.

"Where are you going?" I managed to say.

"Out." That was all she said before leaving.

"Babe, let's go. We'll be late." I waved goodbye to my parents and left.

Thinking about what was to come, we drove off into the night.

"Hey babe, don't worry. You'll be just fine. Isabelle will love you, and so will my parents."

I sighed as Kataon pushed the door open. We made our way to the kitchen, where I saw a lady cooking.

"Ella, I'd like you to meet someone."

She stopped what she was doing and walked over to us.

"Ella, this is Thania, one of the twins I've been telling you about. This one here is my girlfriend, and the other one is Travis's girlfriend."

"Very nice to meet you, Miss. I'm Mrs. Stefanio, but you can call me Ella."

After hearing Ella speak, I picked up on an accent, as if she was of mixed races.

"Mexican. ¿Hablas español?"

"Sí. ¿Hablas español?"

"Un poco más."

"Sí."

Kataon was looking at us as if he had seen a ghost.

"Don't even bother to ask," I said, laughing as Ella went back to what she was doing.

"I was going to." I chuckled.

"Is that my beloved cousin?" Turning my attention toward the voice, I saw a girl about our age. She had dark hair, almost black but not quite there yet.

"Oh hey, Belle. This is Thania, my girlfriend. Thania, this is my favourite cousin, Isabelle."

"Hey, nice to meet you," I greeted her. "Nice to meet you too, and please call me Belle." She hugged me and gave me a smile.

"This way," she gestured toward a room, and Kataon took my hand and entwined our fingers, leading me behind Belle.

We came to a room with a buffet-sized table and a table set for six.

Kataon's parents were already seated, awaiting our presence.

"Shania?"

I looked up to see Kataon's little sister.

"No, this is Thania, her twin."

"Oh. Kataon talks about you every day."

I couldn't do anything but laugh. She was so cute.

I looked up at Kataon, who was busy talking to his mom.

"Hey there, darling. Nice to see you again." Mrs. Miller was wearing a red dress that lay well on her remaining curves.

We hugged, and she gave me a seat beside her.

I greeted Mr. Miller after taking my seat.

Mr. Miller sat beside Mrs. Miller, Kataon's little sister between her and Belle, where Kataon and I sat across from them.

About a minute after talking about random topics, Ella came with dinner. We sat there for about an hour, eating and talking. Again.

An hour later, Kataon asked to excuse us so he could take me home. The car ride was silent and boring, and I wished he'd say something.

Finally arriving at my doorstep, he got out of the car and opened the door for me. He still didn't say anything, so I decided to speak.

"Belle seems nice."

"She is."

He finally walked me to the door, where he kissed me on the cheek and whispered,

"Dream about me, baby doll."

With those words, he drove off.

Leaving my mind saying nothing but, I will.

Chapter 15

K ataon's POV

I was definitely not a morning person. I woke up to the rays of sunlight hitting my face which came from the window.

I got up and make my way to the bathroom then got dressed.

I got news last night not only was Belle was going to live here, but she was also going to go back to school, knowing I had a huge secret about Belle I didn't want to get out to a particular person, I Didn't know how to feel.

Heading downstairs, I saw Belle already dressed for school sitting around the kitchen island talking to Elle.

"What do you want for your breakfast sir"

"Thanks Elle a PBJ would be just fine".

I appreciated everything Elle did for me. I knew her ever since I was a tiny baby, and she was like a second mom to me. I asked her repeatedly not to call me sir, but does she listen... No, she doesn't.

"Here you go sir " she placed the sandwich in front of me, along with a glass of orange juice.

About a minute later my parents came down accompanied by Faith dressed in her school uniform.

"Good morning mom and dad. Belle let's go and thank you Elle".

I kissed Faith on her forehead and went out on my bike with Belle driving my car behind me since she didn't have her own car. I didn't have a problem with giving her my car and use my motorcycle.

I arrived at school and Belle was glad to see the gang again.

Saving me from Travis and his gibberish, the bell rang.

Making my way over to English class, I stopped at my locker and shoved everything into it. I slammed the locker shut I thought it was going to fall off.

"What did it do to deserve that?" I smiled at the familiar voice and slowly turning around to face her.

"Are you just going to stand there smiling like an idiot or say something". By this, she was laughing. I couldn't help but smile even wider.

"Walk you to class?".

"Sure".

"Mr. Miller, is there something you'd like to share with the class?". Mrs. Smith asked.

The class went silent.

"Yes, as a matter of fact yes I would".

She stood there in silence.

"Well, you see, there's this girl" upon saying this, the entire class was whispering to each other. "I think I want to do something nice for her, I was just asking my friend here". I gestured towards Blake. " Idea about that for my girlfriend".

By now, the entire class was whispering to each other.

"I see Mr. Miller. Make sure she's the one because of the rumors, you have quite a reputation with the ladies".

By now even Blake was laughing.

"Let's get back to the lesson now shall we".

"Hey Kataon" I turned around to see Hanna. " We need to talk".

"Sure, meet me at lunch".

"So how are the projects going do far?" Mrs Smith asked.

Shit. I totally forgot about that.

It was finally lunch time and I wanted to know what Hanna wanted to say to me.

Entering the cafeteria, I scanned the room for the one person I wanted to see right now buy unfortunately she wasn't there neither was her Twin.

I went and took a seat between Blake and Travis, neither girls were here.

"Something here is strange"

"Yea tell me about me it, where are the girls?" I asked answering Travis.

But before he could say anything, there was Hanna standing in front of us. She kissed her boyfriend and then I heard somebody faked gagged causing the entire table to laugh.

She stood up and walked over to me then motion towards the door. I got up and she led the way with me following closely behind her.

We stopped as soon as we came up across empty classroom.

We both got in and clear the door. Hanna sat in a chair, and I just stood there waiting for her to speak.

"So what's this" since she wasn't going to break the silence, I figured I would.

"Look Kataon, Thania is a nice girl, and she deserves much better than this so if she's afraid to do certain things, I understand but don't go hurting her. I've only known her for so long but she's a friend nonetheless"

I had no idea what she was talking about.

"If you knew you were going to hit up Kamera why didn't you just leave her alone. What about after meeting your parents and hers all this while you were pretending, I should have known".

I said nothing but look at her, this time I was more than lost, I was clueless.

"What are you talking about. Where is Thania? why didn't she come to me or better yet Shania".

She scuffed up what I said.

"What's going on? Why aren't you guys at lunch"

"You really don't know do you?"

"Know what?' I asked her furious as if I was about to rip her head off.

"Ok. It's this, when you walked Thania to class this morning, Kamera happened. She sent Brooke to do her dirty bidding. Somehow Brooke came up to us and showed us a picture of Kamera texting you".

"I haven't texted that girl since Summer".

At this point, I knew it was nothing good. Nothing good could ever come from Kamera unless it benefitted her or her goons. She was such a bitch.

Standing there in silence, Hanna took her phone out and went on her Instagram profile and clicked on a picture.

"Here" she said shoving it to me. "Read!" She yelled

I looked down on her phone and started to read, I was more than pissed, I wanted to kill that bitch by skinning her alive.

I was going to kill her.

I gave back Hanna her phone and stormed out of the classroom. As I was so mad, even if a teacher came across me, I sure was going to be expelled.

Storming back into the cafeteria I scanned the entire room.

Now's where that bitch.

CHAPTER 16

After standing at the door still looking for Kamera, I finally found her.

I walked over to her table and I could feel the entire cafeteria staring at me.

"Kamera!" I shouted causing her to jump in fright.

"How could you possibly stoop so low. Can't you get it in that thick head of yours that we will never be together".

By this moment, the entire cafeteria was silent.

"Huh?. What in that is hard to understand. You'll never be my girlfriend. No matter what you do, you'll never be my girlfriend. I can never date an insecure, stuck up, little bitch like you".

She said nothing but looked at me. She looked as if she wanted to cry but a smile was plastered on her face.

"And you" I turned towards Broke who looked as if she wanted to run an scream for her life.

"I didn't do it" she said stuttering.

"Then if you didn't post it, then why is it on your page" I answered as a matter of fact.

She said nothing but look at Kamera. Number 3 was silent.

"You little bitch".

This time she finally said something.

She jumped up out of her seat and shoved me. I swear if she wasn't a girl, she'd be on the floor with a bloody nose by now.

"So what huh?. So what if I did it?" She asked as if she was proud of what she did.

"Who are you to judge me". She scuffed and I stood there furious as ever.

"Huh?. Who are you to judge me, definitely not God. And look is calling me a bitch. Little Miss Thania must be something huh, for you to get like this. Tell me something is she that great in bed?"

By that time, I wanted to hit her so bad.

"You bitch". I was never the type to abuse women, emotionally or physically but she deserved it.

I wanted to rip her head off.

"Bitch. Is that how you put it, but can I ask you 1 question, when was it that you found out I was bitch. Before I was on top of you all summer or was it after"

The entire cafeteria let out more whispers at what she said. At this rate I wanted to murder her.

I clinched my fist as if I was going to punch her, but knowing it's wrong to hit a girl, I didn't.

"You want to know when I found out you were a Bitch. The night you begged to go on your knees".

With nothing further, I left the cafeteria in search of Thania, but to my bad luck, she was nowhere to be found .

Thania's POV

I gentle pushed the door to my mom's new cafe for the first time since it was open.

My hands were all wet from rubbing the tears away from my eyes .

"Hey " I herd somebody said causing me to turn around.

"Your Thania right?".

"Yes and you are?" I asked confused as hell.

"Kevin from the party".

Suddenly, it all came back to me.

"Oh my god!" I snickered. "Kevin".

I didn't notice him at first I guess it was because he was now just wearing a Polo shirt along with a black pants and sneakers.

"Hey cute uniform" he said causing me to laugh.

"So what brings you here?" I asked .

"Oh it's lunch at my school and a friend and I decided to come get lunch here , the food is really good, you should try it. And the cakes". He added a moaning sound. " They are to die for".

"Thanks I'll let my mom know to keep up the good work".

"Oh your mom's the owner?" He asked.

"Yes she is and I'll be right back".

I dismissed myself and went to the back were I saw my mom talking to some guy .

"Hey mom" I said in the sweetest way I could.

"Thania sweet heart. What are you doing here?" She asked knowing I was supposed to be at school.

"I had no more classes for the day so I decided I'll come here since no one's at home " I lied.

"Ok well as you can see am busy but have a cup cake or two and if you need anything, I'll be right around the back" .

When my mom said have a cup cake or two, my smile went ear to ear. Mom knew how much I loved her baking so instead of taking two, I took a whole box of 6 and made my way over to Kevin.

"Hey " I said waving at the guy sitting beside Kevin or should I say in front of me.

"Oh Thania this is Roger my boyfriend and Roger this is one out of my twins Thania".

Roger held up his hand for me to shake it and so I did.

"Were you crying?" Roger asked.

I let out a sigh and explained everything to them.

About five minutes into our talking, my phone rang. Again, for about the hundredth time.

"Someone really wants to talk to you" Roger said looking at me.

"Yea I know but I don't wanna talk to them".

"Maybe he wants to explain " Kevin said looking at me.

I did nothing but sigh.

Then suddenly coming in, I herd the one voice I didn't wanna hear. Kataon.

What was he doing here.

"Hey isn't that him" Kevin said pointing over a Kataon.

"Don't point". I said slapping him on the finger.

"Oh god he looks pissed" Roger was now staring with Kevin.

"Oh god he's coming over here".

"Wait what ". But before I could run for it, Kataon was already there furious.

"You " he said looking at Kevin.

"What are you " he asked pissed as ever.

"Some guy trying to hit on my girl". I stared at him hearing his words. What does he mean ' my girl ?.

"Look man I don't want your girl cause she not my type" he said it as if Kataon was supposed to know it already.

"And I'm nothing but gay" he said kissing Roger.

CHAPTER 17

I didn't know what to believe anymore. The fact that I was stupid enough to believe him or the fact that I actually trust him.

Breaking my thoughts, I heard a knock on my door.

"Thania , it's me".

I seriously didn't want to talk to anyone especially Shania.

"Go away".

Instead of listening, she pushed the door and poked her head in.

"I'm your twin, remember. You can't get rid of that easily".

I did nothing but sigh.

"Oh my god. How do you even see?"

She went to the windows and parted the curtains for the light to show in the room and after the light hit my eyes, I hissed like when a vampire comes in contact with light.

"It's been two weeks. All you do is go to school, hide from everyone including cheer practice, you hardly ever show, and coach is all up in my ass about it. You don't sit with us at lunch anymore, anytime dads not working, you let him pick you up instead of waiting on me, you don't even go to the cafe, your friends are asking about you, when your home, you don't come out unless it's for dinner where you hardly speak. What is wrong with you?".

I said nothing. Even though I know she's right. I just don't know what to say.

"You're not even listening, are you?".

"Actually no, I stopped at the part where you were saying something about coach and your ass". I laughed at her.

"You seriously need to get out of this house, it's a Saturday for Christ's sake".

She got up, kissed me on my forehead and left.

I knew she was right, that was the worst part about it.

I dropped my head back down in my bed lazily.

Throwing the covers over me, I let my mind drift back to the night it all happened.

Flashback

"Kataon". I looked up at his messy blonde hair which was now all over the place.

"What are you doing here?" I asked with what little strength I had in me.

"Thania am sorry, please talk to me, I've been looking all over for you".

"You obviously didn't look hard enough, now what do you want?" I asked as if i wanted to cry.

"I think we're going to go". Travis said looking up a me.

"It was nice meeting you Thania. I hope I'll see you at my party week after next week Saturday".

They said nothing more but left my mom's cafe hand in hand.

"I swear to you that I had no idea about what Kamera posted on Instagram. That was not me texting her. I swear to you".

I scuffed, looked up at him and spoke. By now, my eyes were swamping with tears.

"That's not you huh? You know something, I want to believe you so bad but the fact that it's all there, I can't. Have you even looked at the picture, she didn't save the name Kataon, it was just your number. So, if wasn't you then please enlighten me about who it was, was it your other half or were you too afraid to tell a nerd like me you never liked me?".

I was shaking by now, literally shaking.

"That might be my number, but that was not me, I swear it to you Thania, I'll never hurt you or do anything to hurt you".

I got up and made my way outside, not wanting my mom to see me crying, and as expected, he came and followed behind me slowly but surely.

"Quit following me". I snapped at him, but he did nothing but stood there and look at me.

"Thania talk to me".

I didn't say anything but sigh.

I literally was out of words; I had no idea what to say.

"What am I supposed to say. Huh? The fact that you told her I was nothing but a nerd who you want to prove can be good in bed or the text where you said I was nothing to you but an easy target?".

"Thania listen to me, I don't know how she got my phone or what, but I know that was not me".

Seriously Thania, stop crying. My inner me was now kicking in.

" I want to believe you but..." I was cut off by Kataon who shoved me up against the wall and was now kissing me as if his life depended on it. It was hungry, yet needy and passionate at the same time.

I tried to push him away, but it was no use he was taller and stronger than me.

Finally pulling away to catch his breath, I was now breathing heavily.

"Believe that I still I want to be with you, believe that I want you as my girlfriend, believe that I didn't send those text, believe, believe the kiss".

I wanted to tell him that I want to believe him so bad, but I just can't.

"I wish I could".

I ran as fast as my feet could carry me, I had no idea where I was going, but I knew I had to get out of here. I heard him calling me back, but I just couldn't answer, as much as how I wanted to, I couldn't.

End of Flashback

I turn in my bed, to the sound of my phone ringing. I looked up at the time which was now saying it was 5:35. I was asleep for 6 hours. Oh my god.

Paying my attention back to the phone, I answered it.

"Hello. Who's it?".

"It's me Kevin"

"Oh hey Kevin what's up?".

" Nothing more than the fact that you promised Roger you'll be at his party tonight, remember?".

Shit, I totally forgot about that.

"Oh shit. What time is it?"

"7 but you have to be there by 6:30".

"Oh, Ohk then"

"Ok send me your address and I'll be there in thirty minutes".

After coming off the phone, I text Kevin my address and finally got up from the bed, I texted my mom telling her I was going to a party and she said OK.

I made my way to Shania's room knowing my wardrobe had nothing party ready.

I took up a black crop top with a black legging and I paired them with the black I bought before moving here.

Finally getting ready, I heard a car pulling up in the driveway, knowing it was Kevin. I ran downstairs, closed the door behind me and hopped in the car.

Buckling my seatbelt, Kevin spoke.

"Are you sure this is Thania and not Shania?" He asked laughing.

I hit him on the shoulder which causes him to laugh even harder.

"Yes, am sure. Now let's go before Roger chops your head off".

"You look hot by the way".

"Thanks" I was now turning red into a tomato.

"If I wasn't gay. I'll totally do you" he started to laugh.

"Well good thing you're gay". I finished with a laugh.

With this, he drove out of my driveway down the road with me thinking about what was in store for tonight thinking about my first hangover.

CHAPTER 18

I could feel the adrenaline pumping through my body.

Here I was sitting in Roger's kitchen finishing my third shot going into my fourth.

"Easy there, you don't wanna have a huge hangover". I looked up to see both Roger and Kevin looking down at me.

"That's the plan". I raised my fifth shot in the air then pour it down my throat and God it hurts.

"Let's go dance", I grabbed both Roger and Kevin by the hands leading them towards the middle where everyone was, I started to dance while they stood there looking at me.

"What, am I that bad of a dancer?". By now I was screaming because of how loud the music was.

"No not really, you're a terrible dance".

"Whatever you say".

I grabbed a hold of Roger and by now even Kevin was dancing. It was so amazing. I've never felt this light and fun in my entire life. Well, it was my first time enjoying a party, my first time dancing at a party and my first time drinking.

It was more than OK, it was amazing.

"I think am going to get another drink".

"You know, the feelings still going to be there when you wake up tomorrow and probably the after that and the day after that and the day after that".

Kevin was now laughing at Roger who sounded like a baby who just lost his candy.

"It's only going go unless you talk to him. What has it been 2 weeks?".

I know he was right but if drinking could help take the feeling away, even if it was just for tonight, I'll be willing to take that chance.

"Actually 2 weeks and 4 days".

Without saying anything else, I walked off not wanting Roger or Kevin to continue this conversation.

I was sitting here for about half an hour, and I can say that I've lost count of how much drink I had.

Countless if you asked me. Getting up from where I was, I stumbled a bit and then got up back.

Getting it off on the dance floor to Megan Trainer's song No. I felt a little dizzy, so I decided to go upstairs an sit down.

Up on reaching upstairs I closed the bathroom door and sat on the seat with a spinning room. After throwing up, I went outside and told myself it was time to go and I would let either Roger or Kevin take me home.

Up on reaching the staircase, I felt someone grab a hold of me.

"Hey darling" I herd a voice said.

"What do you want" I answered.

"Just be quite and it'll all be over in a minute "he said rubbing his hands through my hair.

And all of a sudden, he gave me a huge push sending me to be up against the wall.

He started to pull his pants down and take my top off.

I started screaming my head off and cursing.

I fought back has hard as I could but, it still didn't make a difference.

Still trying to get him off me, I started to use my fingernails to fight back. Holding my neck to one side he started to kiss me all over my neck.

"Get the fuck off her right now "I heard somebody yelled.

I looked up to see one yelling and another standing there with their fist clenched.

"Yea, or what!"

Now this guy was just pushing his luck.

"I'll show you".

By now, both of them was throwing punches at the guy.

"If you touch her again, I'll break it this time".

One was wringing the guy's hand while the other was holding his throat up against the wall.

Finally letting go, the guy ran down the stairs as if he was mad.

Truth be told, I had no idea who helped me, all I know was that I was now hitting a hard surface.

Maybe I had one drink too many, just maybe.

Kataon's POV

Sitting at home thinking about those 2 ½ weeks, was the worst part of my life.

I still hadn't figured out a way to prove to Thania that I did nothing wrong, and I still had no idea what she was talking about.

Shania didn't talk to me and so did Thania.

The only way I knew what was going on with her was when I saw her in homeroom, when Hanna or Joanna told me about what was going on with her and or when I had football practice where she was practicing in the gym.

Breaking the thought I was in, my phone vibrated.

It was 12:30 in the night, who the hell could this be.

I need you help - Luke

Why the fuck would Luke be texting me this late at night, why'd he need my help.

Dude I'm serious - Luke

What was this dude's problem.

The last time Luke texted me so late about helping him, he needed condoms.

Who the fuck texted someone about condoms in the middle of the fucking night.

Again, my phone vibrated.

But thank God, it was Hayden.

Call me now, we need to talk - Hayden

Finally, someone with sense.

Dialing Hayden's number, I pressed the send button.

"Hey dude. What's up?".

"We need to talk, meet me outside your house".

"Hayden what is this all about?". I ask him.

I could hear a girl blabbering in the background of the phone.

"Just meet me".

I got up and made my way downstairs, opening the door, I was almost scared to death by Isabelle.

"Sup cous, were you're going?".

"Jesus Belle".

She was now laughing hard she started to put a hand on her belly.

"Oh god Kataon. Did I startle you. I'm so sorry".

Note the sarcasm.

"Yea whatever".

"Your phone just got a message".

Looking at my phone, it was Hayden.

Open the door I'm outside - Hayden

Opening the door, I saw Hayden looking all wet and the alcohol was smelling all over him.

"Oh, hey Belle".

"Hayden". she spoke.

"Uhm. You called?". I said as he turned back to me.

"Oh yeah, this way".

Leading me towards his car, I saw Luke leaning against the car.

"Hey man. What's up?".

"Alot". Luke said.

"So, what are you guys doing here? ".

Opening the car door, Luke spoke

"We didn't know where to take her. You're the first person I could think of".

Sitting inside passed out, was Thania.

CHAPTER 19

Thania's POV

Laying still on the bed, I felt pain rushing all over my body. From my head, straight down to my feet.

Finally fluttering my eyes open, I looked up in the ceiling to face a beautiful chandelier hanging.

Oh my god, were am I. My room doesn't have a chandelier, my house doesn't have a chandelier.

Finally looking around, I spotted on the chair some clothes and a note saying Shower an wear me.

Talking the clothes up, I spotted another note on the bed side table.

On it was a cup of water and a pill. This time the note said Take me.

Taking the pill, I searched for the bathroom.

About half an hour later, I came out with a towel wrapped around me humming to the song of Fake Love by Drake .

"Oh my god I love that song"

I swear to god by now I was screaming.

"Hey . It's just me".

Finally realizing I wasn't being kidnapped I looked up to see Isabelle.

Kataon's cousin.

"Oh hi Isabelle, do you mind telling where I am"

"Oh your at our house".

I couldn't come to terms with what she was saying. Did she say our house as in she and Kataon.

"No biggy".

She shrugged.

"What do you mean no biggy. My mom's going to kill me, and the one person am trying to avoid for almost three weeks now I end up at their house all drunk".

"Wait what do you meant by avoid for three weeks? What's up with you guys? And don't worry your mom called and I told her that you were staying at my house, and you'll be home tomorrow".

I said nothing but look at her.

"And you still haven't answered my questions. What's up with you an K?".

"Look Belle I really don't wanna talk about it now. Maybe a next time, I promise".

"Ok but your gonna have to tell me everything. Now lets go get something to eat".

Finally reaching downstairs with Belle, I was greeted by Ella.

"Buenos dias miss Harris".

"Buenos dias Ella".

Isabelle started to look at the both of us.

"Taking Spanish as a freshman came very handy".

"This way senoritas".

Ella led us to the kitchen.

Where I saw Hope sitting on the counter top clapping her hands happily.

"What is she so happy about?"

"Does she need one". Belle replied with a little grin.

"So what do you ladies want for breakfast?".

"Pancakes and bacon with some hot chocolate please". Belle said

I started to grin at her.

"What!. Am hungry".

"And what about you miss Thania"

"Huh. Surprise me".

About a minute later, Ella came with our breakfast.

"Thank you".

She smile and nod then went off to attend to Faith.

Chit chatting with Belle, I looked up from my conversation about a minute later to see Kataon.

I didn't know what I was feeling, angry because of what he did or hurt because I actually liked him.

Finally speaking, he turned towards Ella.

"Hey Belle, uhm Ella may I have my breakfast in my room". Now he was looking at me.

"Ok but just this once, I cleaned that room last night".

Finally finishing my breakfast Ella took the plate from the bottom of us.

"So what now?".

"Home. Mom and dad must be going crazy, where's my phone?".

"Upstairs", she said pointing up.

I got up from where I was sitting and made my way upstairs.

Didn't think someone was inside, I pushed the door open.

"Oh my god, am so so so sorry. I didn't know anyone was in here that's why I didn't knock, I came for my phone and..."

I was cut off by Kataon before I could finish.

"Thania it's OK".

He said in a low tone of voice as if he was sad.

Oh my god, I can't breathe. I'm actually seeing Kataon half-naked. He was dripping wet with a towel wrapped around him.

I went over to the bedside table and took my phone up.

Oh god. I had like a hundred messages.

Some from Roger and Blake also from Hanna and Joanna.

But to my surprise, none from Mom or dad.

As I got up from where I was sitting, I was making my over to the door, Kataon got in front of me and close it.

He had now cornered me in front the door with his two hands on both sides of me.

He was panting. As if he had just ran 20 blocks.

"I didn't do it Thania. I swear to you".

I said nothing but held my head down.

"I can't take the feeling anymore. I hate seeing you smile and can't share it with you".

All of a sudden, our lips were together. Kissing me angrily, it seems as if he was asking for permission. Opening my mouth, I gave it to him.

Kataon tongue was now swishing all over in my mouth.

He pulls away angrily.

Panting, he finally spoke .

"I'm going to prove it to you that I didn't send those messages, I'll never do anything to hurt you". After that, he kisses my forehead and walk away.

Leaving me all speechless and shocked.

"Thania!!" I heard Belle yelling.

"Coming".

I grabbed the door and open it frustrated.

"I'll give you a drive".

Half and hour later, Belle and I arrived at my driveway.

Both cars were gone signifying that no one was home.

"Thanks. Wanna come in?".

She nodded her head silently.

I shoved the door open to the empty house and made my way towrds the kitchen, there I found a note eith writing scribbled on it.

I got the message from your friend about you sleeping over. Glad you're socializing with friends. Gone to the diner.

I sighed softly and set for upstairs with Elle following slowly behind me.

About hour and a half later, Belle and I was now leaving after what seemed like the entire day.

Getting in her car, she started the engine, she was still silent. Damn, the entire car ride to my mons cafe was silent.

"Is there something you'd like to say".

I didn't know what was going on but the Belle I saw this morning was not here with me.

Looking at me, she finally spoke.

"I had sex with Luke".

CHAPTER 20

It has been a full blown week since Kataon and I kiss, Belle had sex with Luke, I last hang out with Roger and Kevin, I last saw Travis and a week since that huge hangover.

"Mom!". I yell from my room.

I was gonna yell for my dad but I forgot he's back at work.

"Shania!".

Now I was frustrated. I hate yelling and got no answer.

"Mother!".

Oh god. I hate this.

Soon after, I saw my mom came rushing in my room.

"What. Is. It?".

She ask panting and trys to catch her breath between each word. She was breathing heavily, almost breathless.

"Sit". I said patting beside me.

"I... I... ". I let out a sigh.

" Please mother, may I have a party next Saturday night?".

I ask finally saying it out loud. I've never asked permission for something like this. I repeat it over and over in my head of how I was gonna ask and it sounds a lot better in my head.

"Uhm". That was all she said before clearing her throat and finally speaking.

"Your dad and I have a business trip next week Friday and we'll be back on Sunday".

Crap then that's a no.

"But if you guys promise not to trash the house it's a yes".

"Thanks mom "I say hugging her.

Two days later

"I can't believe you're throwing a party" Hanna says taking two of my fries and shoving it in her mouth.

"I so can't believe it either" Joanna chipped in.

As I was about to answer, I heard loud noises, and I looked up to see the boys coming in.

Blake is the first one to reach, whereas he sat down next to Amber and kiss her.

"Hey babe" she says retuning the kiss. "Party next week Saturday at Thania's".

As soon as she said those words, I felt Kataon harden beside me.

"I'll be their babe". I heard somebody said and I turned around to see Travis smiling at me.

"I have to go".

I sat up and made my way towards my locker.

Walking off, I came face to face with the hard floor and behind me, I heard snickering of girls.

Finally getting up, I came face to face with the one person I hated right now, Kamera.

"Next time you think twice before going next to Kataon".

I said nothing but scuffed.

"Bitch what are you five?" I yell at her.

I felt a had hit me across my face.

I can't say I wasn't surprised.

My books flew all over the floor and before you know it, I returned that slap right across Kamera's face.

I heard grasp from students standing by, but I didn't care.

Hitting me again, I shoved her against the lockers causing a loud crash.

Holding her sleeves, I continuously shoved her up against the locker.

Holding on to my hair, she grips it and shoves me hard. Walking towards me, she started to hit me and hit me really hard.

Getting a good aim, a slapped her causing her to fringe.

"Bitch".

I scuffed as I am now on top of her, hitting her endlessly.

"I. Hate. You". I scream in between hits.

All of a sudden, I felt two hands wrapped around my waist taking me off Kamera.

Kicking and screaming, I was thrown over a shoulder.

I realized it was him.

"Kataon let me go, put me down"

Finally coming in contact with solid ground, I caught my balance.

He was now staring at me.

"What huh? What?".

He still said nothing.

I let my emotions got the best of me and by now I was crying.

Leaning up against the locker, I slide on the floor, my knees were up to my chest and my chin resting on my knees.

I was crying nonstop.

"What happened back there?".

"She..she..". My hands were shaking as I rock back and forth.

"Hey. It's going to be ok. We'll get to the bottom of this soon".

He leaned forward and kiss me on the head.

Soon his tongue was in my mouth. It felt good. Kataon and I hadn't kiss in like forever. Even though we weren't friends, I missed it.

Hearing someone cleared their throat, I looked up to see Joanna.

"As much as how I love to see you guys like this, now isn't a good time".

I wipe the tears from my eyes and stood up.

"Where're the others?" I ask her following behind her with Kataon behind me.

"The office".

"All of them?".

" Kamera told Mrs. H that it was Shania who you she got in a fight with since she didn't know you guys different and as for Hannah, Amber and Belle, they got friendly with Brooke and Stephanee".

"Let's go".

We arrived there the other boys and I saw everyone else but Travis.

"Hey guys, where's Travis?".

"I have no idea" Hayden replies with his arms wrapped around Johanna's waist.

"Are you boys supposed to be in class?".

We were startled by Mrs. H voice.

"And you young ladies with me right now".

She turned her heels in the opposite direction.

Johanna kiss Hayden goodbye after which the boys left for class and us following Mrs. H to her office.

Walking pass the receptionist, we entire into Mrs. H office.

There was bickering all over, I could hear Amber's voice on top.

"Ladies. Please get a hold of yourself".

Mrs. H was practically shouting. I've never heard her that loud before.

"Now can someone please tell me what happened?". She asked sitting down.

By now the nine of us was quiet.

"We'll start with you Miss Shania".

She gestured towards me.

Didn't want the commotion, I pretended to be Shania.

Shania was now laughing.

Explaining what happened to her, she let Johanna, Belle, Stephanee, Amber and Hanna go.

"Now Kamera, what is your side of the story?".

"She hit me first Mrs. H".

I scuffed knowing that she was lying.

"You have something you want to say Shania?".

"Yes Mrs. H. She's lying. She tripped me and that's how it began".

"Mrs. H can I say something please?". Shania asks.

"Go ahead".

"Look I had no idea how it started, all I know was that I saw my twin sister on the floor, and I got mad, so I started to hit that life-size Barbie doll over there. Now please may I know my punishment so I can go to my Calculus class. My boyfriend might be worried".

Mrs. H was just staring at her as if she was a ghost or something. I've known Shania all my life, since I was in my mom's tummy and even, I was shocked by her outburst.

"Two days detention for you ladies and as for you Miss Thania it's a week and Kamera, one week at home will let you reconsider before you trip someone next time. Now ladies please, leave".

CHAPTER 21

"I so can't believe that you're coming to spend the rest of the week" - Me

"I know right. I so can't believe it either. I get to spend a whole three days with my two favorite persons in the world" - Kevin

"Ahh... I'm touched (holds heart). I love you too" - Me

"Actually, I was talking about Shania" - Kevin

"(Wipe tears), that hurts" - Me

"Lol. Jk. Ttyl Rogers on the line got to go" - Kevin

"Ok see you tomorrow. Pick me up" - Me

After all that happened with Mrs. H, mom was pissed at us. I thought for sure she was going to say no to the party and shipped us off to nanna for the weekend, but instead she took away the car for the rest of the week. So, Travis will be taking Shania and as for me, I had no idea how I was going to go, but am lucky, I guess.

Ok when I say lucky, I mean lucky because I thought I'd had to ask Kataon but soon after mom told us our punishment, we had dinner then she sends us to bed early.

Upon reaching my room, I text Kevin about my party and how he was supposed to spread the word about it.

Anyways lucky there academy would be visiting our school for the rest of the week.

So he's gonna be there from tomorrow which is Wednesday till Friday.

Not only him but Roger and a few others. So here is Kevin saving me from asking Kataon to take me to School.

Instagram was boring and I mean so boring.

Scrolling through my search, I came up Brooke's profile. She was the one that posted the picture of the messages.

I hadn't seen it and I figured I would.

Looking at the messages on the picture, I screenshot it. I also had a chance to read few of the comments.

I wanted to cry but I wasn't going to.

I had no tears left to cry.

"Shania!" I yelled across towards her bedroom.

There was no answer.

"Shania!" I yelled again.

I still didn't get an answer.

Getting up from my bed, I made my way over to her room. Pushing the door, I almost died.

"Thania, please don't scream nor yell nor call mom".

"Travis?".

I was shocked. Shania sneaked Travis in.

Oh. My. God.

"Thania. Please".

"Ok ok I won't say anything" she let out a sigh of relief. "On one condition".

She was now looking at me worried.

"Look at this picture", I showed her the screen shot I took of the messages.

"Thania, why are you showing me this, the more I see it, the more I want to kill Kataon along with that life-size Barbie doll".

"Yea I know but look at the time the messages were send", I said pointing at the time.

"Yea so?". She ask.

"Now look at the date" I said also pointing at the date.

"And this is supposed to make since why?" She asked clueless.

"What date is it?" Travis ask, finally speaking for the first time since I've been in the room.

"October 8". I replied.

" Wait the 8 of last month right?". I nodded my head in reply.

"That's the night I took you to Greenies" he said pointing at Shania. "Remember when I asked about Thania and you said she was having dinner with Kataon and his family".

" Yea I remembered" Shania said surprised.

"The time the messages was sent was 7:12", I said walking up and down Shania's room. "We were having dinner". I replied surprised.

"Kataon's phone was no where around, he lost it ".

"That explains why he was furious when we got back from practice the day before. He couldn't find his phone. I remembered because I gave him my spare. Then there days later, it mysteriously came back".

"Oh my god, Kataon didn't do it" I sighed in relief.

"He didn't do it and all this time I shut him out". I sat on Shania's bed and let out a sigh. "Oh my god, I have to go guys".

"Uhm. Your forgetting one thing, we can't leave the house remember".

"Oh shit, I forgot".

"Use my window". I was speechless.

"You want me to climb out there" I said pointing at Shania's Windows.

We're upstairs while mom and dad is down stairs.

"I'll help you ", Travis said looking at me.

"You would?" I ask.

"Yea it's the least I can do for you not telling your parents I sneaked in and plus I've known Kataon all my life. I'd do anything to see him happy".

"Ok give me a minute".

I left both Travis and Shania in her room and make my way to mine.

Changing out of my clothes, I put on oversized T-shirt and shorts with my black shoes I got from Aunty Pepper.

Soon after, I texted Kevin.

"Come pick me up two houses down from mine. I've got an emergency " - Me

"It's almost ten. This better be worth it" - Kevin

"It is. I promise, explain when you're here" - Me

"Be there in fifteen" - Kevin

Oh my god, I can't believe am sneaking out. It was my first and of course I felt guilty.

"Ok let's go". I said looking up at Travis.

"Thank God it's finally over" I said sighing. I looked up at Shania's windows while brushing off my butt.

Did I mention that's where I land, yes on my butt.

"Hey" Travis says grabbing a hold of me.

"Don't ever stop trying and don't ever give up on him".

"I won't".

With no further words, I ran down the street towards Blake who's sitting patiently in his car.

"So what's this all about?" He asked starting the car and driving off.

"Kataon, he didn't do it" I said in a relief tone of voice.

"So that's were we're going".

"Yes now can you please drive faster".

"Ok darling. We'll be at your lover boy in 20".

I saw a smirk plastered on his face.

"What?" I ask.

"Nothing you have to worry about".

I smiled at him.

"Should I wait for you or should I go?" Kevin ask.

We had just pulled up at Kataon's house. I got out of the car and saw that there was only one car parked in the driveway.

"Yea, Incase he's not here".

knocking, I didn't hear anyone, I tried again and still no answer.

I tried the door and it was open so I made my way to Kataon's room.

"Oh god" I herd somebody half yelled.

"Oh fuck" this time it was a female voice.

Peeping in the room that was half open, tears came to my eyes.

Running downstairs, I ran out of the house as fast as I could.

I got into Kevin's car crying as fast as I could.

"Drive!" I yelled.

The car was not move, I thought I said drive.

"What happened?" Kevin ask.

"I said drive!" I said yelling as hard as I could and this time, he was driving.

Finally coming to a stop, I looked up to see my house.

"So are you going to tell me what happened?".

I sighed.

"Ok this is what happened..." I told Kevin everything that happened while crying in his arms.

I felt so stupid.

I hate him.

I. Hate. Kataon. Miller

CHAPTER 22

"Mom, dad later" I ran into the kitchen and took up a breakfast muffin mom made and an apple to go after which I rushed out the door towards Kevin's car.

"Hey Travis" I said before getting in.

"Shania should be done any minute now".

"Ok thanks" he said before Kevin drove off.

"Hey Kev, wassup Roger?" I spoke.

"Nothing much, I have seen you since my party are how you?"

"I'm good" I lied.

"Lies!" Kevin shouted.

"Is there anything I need to know?" Roger asked all clueless.

"She walked in on lover boy having sex" he said laughing.

"You what. Oh my god" he was surprised. "Are you OK?"

"Yea I guess" another lie.

The truth was, I was hurt, I wanted to lock my room door shut and never come out of it.

I wanted to scream so badly but I can't, I don't want him to think that I'm weak or anything, so I just have to hold it in.

"Oh my god girl" Kev squeal. "Your school is so cute" this time he got out of the car. "Only one problem though" he said frowning.

"And that's?" I asked getting out behind Roger.

"How the fuck am I gonna know you different, the girls are all wearing the same thing"

"That's why it's a private school you dummy" I said laughing.

"How do you know Roger at your all boys private school" I said mimicking his word private.

"Yea whatever"

"Let's go" I said laughing.

We all walked in the hallway towards my locker.

On my way there, I saw other boys from Roger and Kevin's school. The boys also got a few stares and stuff from the girls here.

"So what now?" Blake ask coming over with Jaiden.

"The auditorium, Mrs H wants to talk to the entire school, even freshmen, so am betting it's about your school being her".

"Hey babe" I heard that familiar voice said along with chartering, and I know that everyone else is behind him.

I felt my body tensed up.

"So, guessing he's more your type" Kataon said pointing at Roger making reference when he first met Kevin at his parent's party.

"So how have you been?" She asks.

"I'm good" he replied. " This is my boyfriend Roger" he said entwining their fingers.

"Hey" Shania said smiling at Roger. "I'm her other half Shania".

"I've figured" Roger said laughing.

"Hey where do I know you from?" Hayden spoke for the first time. "What's the name of your school?" He asks.

"Isaac's Academy" Roger replied.

"Oh, I know" Luke said. "You play ball".

"Yepp" Roger said popping the p.

"You're their QB?" Jaiden said but it sounded more like a question.

"Yes, I am the QB" Roger said.

"A gay QB. That's new" Jaiden said causing Joanna to elbow him.

"So where were you two last night? Jaiden ask pointing at Kataon and Travis.

"I have to go" I said.

"I'll see you guys in homeroom".

"What's wrong ?" Hanna ask.

"I'll be ok" I replied shuting the locker.

"You sure" Belle said.

"Yea am sure".

"Ok but I need to talk to you about what I told you last week. I think". Belle said. " Come over?".

"I can't. Sorry" I felt like crying. "I'll see you guys".

I turned the opposite way and started to walk as quickly as possible without anyone noticing I wanted to just leave.

"I'll see you guys" Kevin said following behind me with Roger.

She wanted me to come over there. I walked in on the guy having sex after telling me that he's gonna prove to me that he didn't do anything wrong. And when I finally found prove, that happens.

I just wanted a go back to his everything was before moving here.

Shania had her old friends back that I secretly hated because of how much black they wore, and as to me, I'd go back to the girl who was always locked up in her room reading books.

I just wanted things to go back to being normal.

I wanted to be normal, that was all am asking for.

"Good morning class" Mrs Allen said as she walked in.

"I'll take the register after which you will exist in an orderly fashion to the auditorium where Mrs Harrington will be address the entire school".

"Hey mom do I have to go?" Hayden ask.

"Yes Hayden you have to go, you might be special to me but at school your just regular student".

Hayden frowned.

After Mrs Allen took the register, we all left the classroom and head towards the auditorium.

"Hey wait up". Hanna said holding on to my shoulder.

"We need to talk"

"Ok sure" I stopped were I was and was joined by Amber, Shania and Johanna.

"So whats this about?" I asked.

"Since you know, Uhm Kamera has been suspended and we don't have a captain anymore so yesterday after practice when you left, we voted for a replacement, and you won". She said squealing.

"Thanks" I said then walk away.

I scanned the entire auditorium for Kevin and Roger and luckily I found them as quick as I can.

"Please be seated" Mrs H spoke through the microphone.

Soon, the entire auditorium was quiet.

"As you all can see, we have visitors. The boys from Isaac's Academy will be staying at your school for the rest of the week to partake in a couple of exercises. Since our two schools are the only two private schools in this area, Isaac's Academy will be the only school visiting. You'll have them in your classes and you'll see them at lunch. Only seniors from there school are here but they'll be in other groups to give a helping hand. Please treat them with equal respect. "

After her long speech, everyone got up and started talking to the boys, mostly just the girls.

"Hey" Roger said touching me.

"I have History next, any idea where?" He ask.

"Yep that's with me" I said.

"I have Chemistry", Kev said.

"That's with me" Shania said.

"Then let's go" Kevin said kissing Roger goodbye.

"See you guys at lunch" he said then left.

Roger smiled happily at Kevin as he left us standing.

Seeing the happiness in Roger's eyes, made me ever wonder if I'll ever find myself that type of happiness.

I wonder if I'll ever find someone that makes me happy.

I want happiness.

CHapter 23

"Is that all your having for lunch" Roger ask

"Yep" Amber replied popping the p.

"She gained three pounds and wants to take them off" Johanna inputs.

"I know the perfect way for you to take it off" Hayden says looking at her smirking.

"Ok then" Shania said disgustingly.

We all sat at our regular lunch table with everyone including the new newbies who is Roger and Kevin.

I managed to get through three classes without saying anything to Kataon. Not even an eye contact.

A part of me was glad and a part wanted to scream I need you.

What the hell am I even doing, am I saving myself from getting hurt or is this torture.

"Earth to Thania" Johanna tells while waving her hand in front of me. Wow I must have zoned out.

"Oh, yea what?"

"Your party still on?" She asks

"Yea it's this Saturday night" Luke said stuffing a few of Joanna's chips in his mouth. "Hey that's mine" she yelled. "Sharing is caring" he smirked.

"Yea. Who said I care?" She asked. "Ouch, that hurts" he said putting his hand over his chest.

"Back to the party" Hayden says.

"What about it?" Amber asks.

"Never mind" Johanna imputed. "Just know I'm coming over"

"Me two" Amber joined.

"And me" there goes Hanna

"Count me in then" way to go Belle.

"Let's just have a sleepover" I said. "Friday night it is then" I finished.

"Thania, remember I need to talk to you" Belle says as I was about to leave.

"Ok. You can come over later".

I left and went straight to my locker.

Shoving my books inside, I was lifted over somebody's shoulder.

"Put me down!" I yelled kicking while the person took my bag up an shut my locker.

Realizing who it was, I stopped fighting.

Feeling myself coming in contact with the ground I looked up to meet those beautiful grey eyes I've been longing to look in.

I know those grey eyes anywhere.

I knew Kataon anywhere.

Kataon's POV

I didn't know it understand what was going on. Breaking the silence, I finally spoke.

"Thania? I said.

She said nothing but looked away.

"What is going on?". She still said nothing.

"Talk to me".

"You want me to talk huh?". I had no idea if she was pissed at me.

"Well then let's talk. I trusted you, I believed that you'd fix things, I believe that so call kiss, I even doubted myself because I taught, I was wrong, and you were right. I taught that I meant something to you. I taught; I taught you actually care".

Hearing what she was saying with tears in her eyes, I felt all her pain.

"I do care". I shouted so she could hear.

"I might not be the best at these so call relationship things but one thing I know is that I want you".

"I don't think so". she answered.

Hearing the anger in her voice made me came to my sense's, she just wasn't talking about what Kamera did, there was something else.

"Is there something that you're not telling me?", I asked.

"Last night, what happened?".

Damn, she knows.

"I... I... I".

She scuffed looking at me while walking towards the door.

Opening, she spoke.

"I didn't thing so".

"Class dismiss".

Walking out of my computer science class, I head straight towards the parking lot.

I didn't know what to tell her, the truth or just lie about it.

I really care for her; I even told my parents how I felt about her. Faith would always trouble me about her while Ella will always ask when she's coming back over.

But sadly, I have no idea what to say.

My mom and dad will he going on a business trip next week for three days and would like to know if she can come over to watch Faith for them.

Getting on my motorcycle, I headed for home.

I couldn't be at school no longer, I knew if I'd stayed, I would do something I regret.

Pulling up in the driveway half an hour later, I shove the door and went towards the kitchen.

"Ella" I called out to see if she was home.

But unfortunately, I got no response.

Taking a bottle of my dad's whiskey, I saw a note in moms handwriting.

Taking it off, I read it aloud:

Hey Kataon, your dad and I left for a short while and will be back on Sunday. Sorry for the rushing, I wanted to let you know myself, but we had to go. Tell Belle about our decision and when we'll back. Ella is at your dad's parents with Faith and will be back on Thursday where the Harrison's daughter will be keeping her, take care of yourself.   Mom.

Great, now this is just exactly what I asked for. Note the sarcasm. How the hell am I going to get something to eat since Ella is not here.

Taking the bottle up to my room, I came back down out of my uniform and search for something to get my mind off the actual situation.

Thania.

Taking up my another of my dad's bottle of vodka, I open the bottle and I went back to my room with the bottle already half down.

By now, I felt free, and the pain was gone, for now.

Closing the door behind me, I dropped myself on the floor.

I felt like crying.

She wasn't smiling at me, she doesn't even look at me, she's having a party and didn't even invite me.

Getting angry, a hit a fist in the wall, as soon as I stand.

"Why won't she look at?". I yelled throwing a beer across the room causing it to smash on the wall.

I just want the pain to go away.

Hitting both fist in the wall I started to throw everything around, by now by sheets where all over and my room looked like trash.

I needed my pain to go away, I need Thania.

CHAPTER 24

Finishing the bottles in my room, I sat down on the ground holding my hair in my hand.

"Get the fuck out of my head" I yelled.

Throwing whatever I could find, I yell. "Why won't she look at me".

"Kataon!" I heard somebody yell from downstairs".

Hearing a knock on the door, the voice spoke again, I finally realized who it was but sadly, it wasn't Thania.

"Go away Belle".

Indeed of doing what she's told, she shoved the door open.

"Oh my god" was all she could utter.

"Get the fuck out" I yelled shoving her out and slamming the door.

I loved my cousin so much but I couldn't let her see me like this. I knew what I just did hurt her, but I had to.

Walking away from the door, I walked over to a far corner and sat. Thinking about her, thinking about my drug, thinking about Thania.

Thania's POV

Stepping into the shower, I rest my phone in the windowpane humming to Ed Sheeran latest song, Shape of you.

About a full half an hour, I finally came out singing I don't wanna live forever by Taylor Swift and some guy I didn't know due to lack of socialization.

"Trust me, it's more than that"

Upon hearing the voice I was shocked. Turning around, I saw Belle sitting on my bed.

"Was I just talking out loud?" I ask.

"Yepp" she replied popping the p.

Putting my clothes on, I lay on my tummy with my feet up in the air.

"So what did you have to tell me?".

She sigh and came beside me.

"Remember how I told you I slept with Luke?" She asked causing me to nod.

"We didn't stop". By now I was speechless

"After it happened the first time, we wanted to stop but we couldn't. I couldn't". I still remained silent.

"What would you do when you accidentally had a one night stand with your first person you had sex with some years ago. I wanted to stop, I really didn't want a relationship like this. But I decided I wanted to give it a try but no sex".

she was now pacing back and forth in my bedroom.

"Until some nights ago when he came over to look for Kataon, who wasn't there, we had a few drinks, watch a movie or two when he told me he wanted to come out of the hiding and let's be a normal couple who goes on dates and stuffs like those. We were having sex a while back and someone walked in on us, I want to be with him, he's the only boy I've ever been with but there's something that I'm hiding from him that happened when I used to live hereBy now , she was crying.

Processing what she said, everything came back to me.

"Wait did you say someone walked in on you guys and ran out after". Still crying, she nod.

Oh my god.

"That was me" I said sounding happy.

I got up from my bed.

"So let's put the pieces together" I said looking at her.

"You had sex with Luke, not once nor twice, Kataon would kill Luke if he finds out, I walked in on the both of you thinking it was Kataon, I broke up with him over it, Luke wants to go public about the two of you sneaking around, you want it but Kataon won't allow it and last but not least Kataon didn't hurt me, I hurt him".

After saying all that, I did nothing but stand in shock with tears.

"Yea" Belle says. " That pretty much sums it up".

I hurt Kataon. He did nothing and I blamed him for nothing he did.

Coming back to reality, u wiped the tears from my eyes and turn towards Belle. I finally spoke.

"So where do I fit in all of this?" I ask her.

"Convince Kataon to let me be Luke. Please am begging you" she begs.

"He won't even look at me anymore" I said crying.

"He's going crazy about you. Literally" she spoke saying the last word si I didn't hear but luckily I did.

"What do you mean literally?" I ask her but didn't get a reply.

"Isabelle" I spoke looking at her.

She still said nothing but look at me.

"Isabelle what's going on?" I ask.

"Nothing" she said a little to unsure.

"You're a crappy liar. You know that right?" I ask.

She sighed looking at.

"Look, I love my cousin, but I've never seen him like this before. He's drinking nonstop. He even took his dad's stash. There's no sign of any alcoholic beverages in the house. There are all empty bottles in his room. What part of it left. His room is a mess, everything is all over, broken glasses, the furniture are broken up all over his room".

I said nothing but let the tears fall.

"Your getting to my cousin's head Thania, he won't look at you because every time you smile and he's not there to share it with you, it tears in him, he loves you Thania, more than you realize. Just please forgive him. Please".

I started to cry more an more. I was a total Bitch. And it was the truth. I hurt him.

"More than ever" Belle says. Which concluded that I spoke out loud.

"I need to see him". I says to Belle.

"Let's go" she says grabbing up her car keys and closing the door behind her.

It was now or never.

I loved Kataon and I want him to know the truth.

I love him.

CHAPTER 25

Kataon's POV

I knew Mom and Dad were considering shipping me off to rehab. My room resembled a crime scene, ransacked and chaotic. I had consumed all of Dad's liquor, beers, and wines.

Despite my efforts, the pain persisted. Her smile, her voice, her presence haunted me relentlessly.

Seated, tears streaming, I heard a voice calling.

"Kataon, are you in there?"

"Belle, get out!" I yelled, gripping my hair.

"Kataon, it's not in your head. Please, open the door," she pleaded, her voice cracking.

"No, it's just... that voice again," I muttered to myself.

Pushing the door, I found Belle standing there.

"Leave, Belle," I ordered.

"Should I go too?" Thania's voice interrupted.

She approached, her hand resting gently on my cheek.

Seeing her tears nearly broke me.

"I didn't do it, Thania. I swear. I didn't send those messages. And the night you asked where I was, I was at the lake, thinking of you.

Please believe me. Kamera means nothing to me. You're the one I love, and I'll fight for us, no matter what."

Tears still streamed down her face.

Her words melted my heart.

"I know you didn't. I'm sorry, Kataon. I love you too."

All I could do was kiss her, desperate to show her how much I loved her.

She loves me, and I love her.

This time, nothing will come between us.

I could have kissed her forever.

A throat clearing interrupted us. I looked up to see Belle.

"There's something I need to tell you," Thania said, her eyes locked on mine.

"Luke," I said, glancing at Belle.

"I'm sorry, cousin. I know you said not to date your friends, but..."

"It's okay," I reassured her.

"I shouldn't have kept you apart all these years. I shouldn't have told Auntie about you two. Maybe if I hadn't, she wouldn't have sent you away to some fancy boarding school, and Luke wouldn't have been such a pain."

"You asshole," a voice interjected. Blood stained my clothes by the time I looked up.

"You did this. I thought you were better than this," I said to Luke.

Luke hit me again.

I didn't want to fight him, knowing it would only escalate.

"Luke, calm down," Belle pleaded through tears.

"We were supposed to be friends. Because of you, I missed seeing them turn into her," he said, pointing at Belle.

"Luke, I know you hate me, but I had to. She's my little cousin. She was too young," I explained, trying to calm him.

"What the hell happened here?" Hayden asked as he entered the room with Travis, Blake, and Jaiden.

"Ask him," Luke said, moving toward me before Belle stopped him.

"Hey, man, what's going on?" Jaiden asked.

"I don't want to talk about it," I said, wiping away the blood.

"If you won't, I will," Luke threatened angrily.

"Remember that end-of-year party freshman year? The truth or sip game?" I asked them.

"Yeah, we remember. The night we played truth or dare and got drunk," Travis recalled.

"Yeah, best night ever," Hayden added.

I recounted the events.

"We didn't know most of the girls, except Belle, who was always with us. Random hookups happened even though we were only sixteen.

"A week later, Luke was acting weird, and somehow you three ended up in lasting relationships, Belle distanced herself, and Travis and I just..."

"Kept on being Travis and me," Travis finished.

"That summer, our parents took a trip to Jamaica and brought us along. Two weeks in, Belle got sick and found out she was four weeks pregnant.

"She told me because she loved me, but being insecure, I told my parents, who told hers. She's hated me ever since, even if she says she doesn't, I can tell she does.

"We got home, and my aunt sent her to an all-girls boarding school, where she gave birth to twins. She left without saying goodbye to me, only leaving a note for Luke saying she wouldn't return.

"Months later, she reached out to me and Luke. I begged my aunt to let her come back, and thankfully she did, with the condition we never speak of what happened.

"The twins are with our grandmother in England until she's eighteen, which is in four months. I know I was wrong and I'm sorry."

When I finished, Belle was crying, and Luke, Hayden, Jaiden, and Travis were speechless. Thania looked at me, unsure of what to say or do.

Silence hung heavy until Luke stormed out, slamming the door. Belle ran after him, and the others left quietly. Thania sat in a corner; her eyes fixed on me.

In that moment, I realized I might lose everything, everyone.

CHAPTER 26

It was finally here, my first party. Mom and dad left early this morning and left us a few rules of their own but Shania and I, we had our own. I couldn't get the party I wanted if I agreed to moms' rules.

"You've been in there for an hour, what's wrong?"

I was locked in the bathroom having a cold feet. What if my party goes down, what if nobody shows up?

I swear I was hyperventilating by now, but to honest I was just nervous.

"Where is that bitch?".

Kevin.

Before I could hear any answers, my bathroom door was already pounding down.

"Girl get your ass out of that bathroom before there is no door left".

" Fine ". I yelled. "I'm coming"

I opened the door and standing before me was a displeased Kevin.

" Why is our hostess not at her own party?".

I sighed.

"Let's go. Chop chop".

Walking downstairs, I spotted the rest of the girls chatting and laughing along with Roger.

" Hey gorgeous " was Amber's first words.

"Hey guys". I let out a smile.

By this time, my so call other half was nowhere to be found.

"Where is Shania?" I asked

"Travis" Joanna spoke out disgust.

*******By this time, my living room was a mess.

Bodies everywhere jumping up and down or couples making out and or drunks all over.

Truth be told, I didn't expect so many persons to be here. They were even boys from Isaac's Academy here. Listening to the music pounding, I was all alone. No one but me.

Or so I thought.

Kataon's POV

Sitting at home with a now clean refurbished room, I streamed on my phone then suddenly I got a text from Travis.

Party at the twins?

To be honest I wanted to go so badly but I seriously don't know what would happen between Luke and me.

I know that I was the cause of what Belle went through, but I was a stupid little boy for telling them like that.

She trusted me and I let her down. I know her parents would have found out eventually, but she begged me to lie for her and tell them that it was a drunken mistake and that she didn't know who the dad was. But no, little me had to spill.

Breaking me out of my thoughts, my phone vibrated again.

I'm outside.

It was a message from Belle.

Opening the door for her, she stepped in.

"Look K I'm sorry about what happen but you have to understand how Luke feels".

I sighed.

"Look Belle I should be the one saying sorry, I was this stupid
kid 2 years ago. Maybe if I hadn't blab about what happened, Luke
would have gotten to know his kids".

She smiled at me and pulled me in for a hug.

"So, what are you up to?"

"Before I answer your question answer mine. Why'd you text me
before you came into my room, or you could have at least knock"

"I know but after what happened, I didn't want to catch you off
guard".

" Where are you going all dressed up like this? ".

" Thania's party. Aren't you going? ".

"I was never invited".

"How come on. So's half the school".

"Now let's go".

About half an hour later, I pulled up at the twins.

Before I could say anything, Belle was already inside.

Not knowing what to do or say once I'm inside, I sat in the car
peaceful.

Sighing, I got out and made my way inside, I was surprised, for
her first party, it was a blast.

"Hey man you came". I turned around to see Shania and Travis.
"Hey, you" Shania smiled politely as if I was a stranger.

"Yea thanks to Belle"

With a wide grin on her face, Belle stood in Luke's arms smirking proudly.

"Hey man" Luke said. "Luke" was my only reply.

"Look man I'm sorry about the other day and I know I was wrong, and you were doing the right thing. If I was in your position, if it was my cousin, I'd do the same thing".

"I'm sorry too I was just foolish and an overprotective little boy, but when Belle needed me the most, I let her down".

" So". Belle looked at the both of us.

"This is forgiven right?" She asked.

"It better be".

I knew that voice anywhere.

"How much of that did you hear?" Shania asks her.

"Enough".

With nothing more, she placed her lips against mine and instantly it felt like forever since I felt her lips against mine.

We were so caught up the moment we forgot where we were until somebody cleared their throat.

Thania's POV

"Enough PDA now let's dance" Then suddenly Joanna came out of nowhere with Hanna.

"Where's Amber" I asked.

"Somewhere getting all knocked over the head by Blake. Speaking of Blake, where's Kevin and Roger?"

Joanna answered my question and asked at the same time.

"Probably being knocked up by too"

Hanna said causing us to laugh.

While dancing, so many thoughts went through my head. Like me kissing Kataon, Belle and her kids and a way to get back at Kamera Taylor.

Finally, I had peace and quiet.

Everyone left expect the guys and the rest of us.

We were all cleaning up, so we didn't have to go through a lot of trouble in the morning.

"Hey guys".

I was busy cleaning to realize it was Amber.

" So, no hey Amber or anything ". she said looking at us when no one replied.

" Oh, Amber hey, I didn't see you I was busy sorry, speaking of busy, where have you been, I haven't seen you all night". Hanna responded sarcastically.

She was glowing.

Looking down she smiled.

"We'll talk later, now grab a broom".

"What time is it?"

Hanna was now sitting on the floor pouting.

"A little after 2". Belle answered.

"We've been cleaning this long" she wined.

"No, we've been cleaning this long while you're just stealing kisses from Jaiden". Belle joked.

We both laugh at Amber's response to her.

Taking out the last bag of garbage, Roger and Kevin walked in.

" And where have the two of you been? " Johanna asks

"Hmm, out" was Roger's reply.

"Oh, I see, we get nothing just an 'out', no little detail no nothing" Shania replied.

"And you miss Amber" Joanna said turning her head towards Amber.

"You don't say Joanna, because I know Thania's room was filled with pleasures"

My mouth fell open.

"So, while I was here enjoying my loneliness, you're all getting it on?".

"Everyone but me" Belle said raising her hand.

"Oh, shut up " Amber replied causing us to laugh.

Interrupting our little moment, Luke walked in followed by the rest of the boys.

"So, this is how it's going to be because nobody's leaving until tomorrow. Ok so Luke and Belle will be in my room along with Haydn and Joanna. In Shania's room you'll have Shania and Travis along with Blake and Amber, Roger and Kevin, the living room is all yours so go get sheets and stuffs while Jaiden and Hanna are with me in the guest room".

" But first am making coffee, anyone want a sip".

"If it comes from your mouth then fine, I'd love to have it".

"You know you only said like 5 words to me since night and now all you can do is come with some cheesy pick-up line". I tsk. "I expect so much from you Mr. Miller, such disappointment" I laughed along with the others.

"How about I put the pretty little mouth of yours to good use"

But before I could answer, his lips were on mine. Causing Amber to gaged.

"Don't you just hate PDA's".

So much for tea.

We all said our goodbyes and headed off to our designated areas.

CHAPTER 27

"Happy Halloween".

I woke up to a smiling Shania.

"Oh Thania cheer up, you know its my favorite holiday"

"And my worst" I imputed

"You always do the worst things on Halloween, remember last year when you put dye in my shampoo, I had green and purple hair for 3 weeks. Even though everyone thought it was cute, I cried for days".

She was laughing at me. I took the pillow and throw at her, but luckily, I missed.

" For a cheerleader, you suck at throwing ".

I showed her my middle finger same time as my dad walked in.

"Hey Pumpkin's" he smiled.

"Hey dad, aren't you supposed to be at work"? Shania asked

"No, I got the day off. I'll be at mom's cafe, so I'll see you guys later". He kissed bout our foreheads and left.

"I'm go to go take a shower" Shania said before she left.

Hearing my message tone, I started to sing along.

"I didn't know that I was starving till I tasted you, don't need no butterfly when you give me the whole damn zoo".

" Aren't you going to pick that up, it's annoying" Shania shouts from across her room.

"Fine".

I took up my phone to see that I got not one but two messages. One from Kataon and one from Belle.

Kataon - Happy Halloween, can I drive my girlfriend to school today.

Replying to Kataon's message, I called over to Shania.

"What is it" she asked

"Kataon's driving me to school today"

"That's ok I'll just have Travis pick me up"

I text mom telling her that we won't be using the car so if she sees it in the driveway, we didn't ditch school.

It was Halloween and one of the little breaks we get from uniforms, so I looked into my closet to decided what I was going to wear to school today when my phone lit up.

All black today- Hanna

We got the chance to wear regular clothes due to the fact that my school apparently goes to some Halloween special at a different school, it consisted of a football game and a few other things and the money from that went to charity.

Coming to a halt, Kataon parked beside the others, it was a routine now. We'd park our cars at the back of the parking lot in a row, now the only car that was missing was Shania and I.

It's been a little over two weeks since the group is back together and Kataon and I are finally a normal couple.

He got out of the car and opened my side letting me out and closing it behind me.

He locked our fingers together while walking over to the others.

"Earth to Thania" Amber said waving her in front of my face.

"Oh hey". I said didn't even realize I spaced out.

"So, what's on the agenda" Haydn spoke.

"Party at my house" Jaiden said.

"Can I ask one question" I said.

"Ask away" Hanna spoke

"Whose idea was it for us to wear all black"

"That would be mine" Belle spoke.

"So, you mean to tell me that the one day since September we get to wear anything but our uniforms to school and you chose for us to wear all black?".

"Yes" her immediately dry reply.

Leaving for no space to argue, the bell rang signally that we have five minutes for classes to begin.

We all made our way into the halls where all eyes were on us.

Travis and my sister in front with Kataon and I behind followed by Belle and Luke, then Blake and Amber, with Haydn and Joanna behind and last but not least, Jaiden and Hanna.

Everyone was whispering by now.

Walking towards us in the opposite direction was Kamera and her two bobble heads. Broke and Stephnee.

"Look who the cat dragged in".

She stopped right in front of us.

" Look like the dead, the full black works for you, it makes you look a little less than trash".

"What did you just say tramp". Hanna said pushing her way to the front.

To be honest, I'd never seen Hanna like that.

"Babe, let it go" Jaiden said going in front of Hanna to block her away from Kamera.

"My my, look who decided to let loose. Little miss perfect"

"Kamera, go or you'll regret ever knowing the name Jaiden Issac".

She took a step back and walked away passing us going about her business.

"Skank" she whispered to me while walking by.

Somehow Shania herd.

"What did you just call her" She shouted.

"Two of a kind" she responded.

By the time Shania could answer, Hanna manages to get away from Jaiden and was all over Kamera.

Soon enough even I wanted to hit her.

"Kataon let go of me", I shouted trying to break loose from him.

But he only held his grip tighter.

Somehow, they all manage to get a hold of us.

Great, now I'll miss first period.

We all sat in an unoccupied classroom with complete silence.

" Why'd you do that?" Jaiden ask Hanna.

"Look babe I'm sorry, but I lost it. I'm sorry but she had it coming".

" Fine but no more fights". he said to her, the rest of us stayed silent.

"Fine".

After agreeing to try and not get into with Kamera, we went straight to class.

" I have a great idea" I said to everyone.

"And that would be"? Joanna asked.

" You'll see but first, I'll have to ask Kataon to help me".

It was now after school, which had ended mid-day for the school's charity, we were sitting on benches watching a game of football.

The event was fun, they had a bouncy house, popcorn and other treats on sale.

We sat through about 3 games, one with the JV and the seniors, the alumni and the JV and of course the seniors and Alumni.

After it ended, I discussed my little trick or treat o them and they agreed but Kataon.

"Babe I'm not doing that. I'm sorry but no". Kataon was pacing up and down in my living room.

" Please ".

" Babe no. I don't want her to think the other way".

I made the saddest face I could and reached out and pulled him on the sofa kissing him and as soon as he deepens the kiss. I stopped.

He let out a loud growl.

"Fine".

I smiled at him and watched him take his phone out texting Kamera on Instagram.

Meet me at the old building on your street at 8. Wanna discuss us. Johanna will bring you and if you tell my girlfriend its off.

" Are you happy now". He looked irritated.

But before I could answer, Kamera had already answered.

I'd love too. Xoxo.

Now we're in for trick or treat.

CHAPTER 28

Kamera's POV

It was all coming back to me know. I was shaking from head to toe, its like it was taking place all over again. I just sat outside all alone thinking about the beginning.

It all started when my little Kataon told me to meet him at this house that nobody was living in for years.

But that didn't matter, anything for my little Kataon.

It all began 24 - 30 minutes ago when Johanna came for me at Jaiden's party, and I decided to take Steph and B along.

"Let's go".

We were standing in front the building, it was old and very old, dark and abandon.

" Is this the place. I'm not going in" B looked all scared.

"What could possibly go wrong. I want to go meet Kataon who's waiting for me". I eyed B up and down.

But to my surprise, everything went wrong.

It was like the opposite of everything.

As we stepped inside, I text Kataon asking where he was.

But to my surprise. He didn't get the massage.

No signal.

" It's Halloween and I want candy". We herd an unknown voice spoke out loudly in a room that only black could be seen.

"Who's there" Johanna spoke out.

"Imagine what it would have been like for Halloween without candies, or should I say screams". The person responds.

Now I was getting scared.

" Who are you, you still haven't answered the question as yet" I decide to speak.

"I. Want. Screams". The only thing we could see was the person holding up a knife with something like blood dripping from it. We couldn't even see the persons face.

B started to scream. Followed by the rest of us.

We ran towards the exit, but it was no use. It was never going to open at this rate. It was shut from outside.

" I like the brunette. She's cute. I think I'll take her".

The person grabbed on to Johanna dragging her as she kicked and screamed.

"She'll be lonely. How about you join her" he now grabbed on to Steph.

"Let go a me" Steph screamed.

"Shut up" the person held on tighter to Stephs hair pulling her.

About 5 minutes of trying to open the door, I decided to try another exit.

"I think I hear someone screaming" B said opening a door.

There we found Steph with her hands and feet tied up with a Halloween mask over her face and in the closet, Johanna was kicking.

She was also tied up by her hands but not her feet. She had on a blind fold.

"We need to get the hell outta here".

Johanna screamed.

" Not so fast" the person stood at the door but as always, we couldn't see there face.

He held up a knife with blood dripping from it.

"What do you want from us".

He tsk.

" Screams" his only reply.

"Now do as I say". He walked in closing the door.

" There's 4 of you in here and 4 chairs. Sit ".

We did as we we're told.

" The blonde, open that closet".

I walked over to it and opened. There was a girl in there all bloody and tied up.

I couldn't recognize her because of the dark.

I started to scream.

"Just like that". He responded but was gone as I turned around.

The four of us immediately got up and ran towards the back.

Luckily, the door was unlocked.

We ran outside towards the front.

There I saw Kataon, Shania, Thania, Hanna, Amber and two guys I didn't know coming out of the same building I was just in.

The girls had red all over them.

Then behind me, Johanna started to laugh.

" I didn't know a blonde could scream that loud" Amber said laughing.

"Neither did I" one of the guys I didn't know laughing.

"You" the only thing I could utter.

"Us" the other guy said.

That's him. The one who was inside.

"That was you. You bitch".

" Don't call my babe no bitch. You little whore" the other guy spoke.

"I taught you wanted me back" I said to Kataon almost crying.

"Want you back" he scuffed. "You're even more pathetic than I thought".

Just then Shania held up the knife and wiped her finger on the blade then licking her finger.

" Ketchup ".

I felt like I could cry.

" Ok. Now can I please go and enjoy my boyfriends party. He's waiting for a dance".

They all walked past me into kataon's and one of the guys I didn't know car which was not there then I first came.

Before they drove leaving Brooke, Stephnee and I, Thania came out the front of Kataon's car.

She turned towards be and spoke.

"Trick or Treat bitch".

Thania's POV

Leaving a scared Kamera behind me, I felt happy.

" who are you and what have you done to my girlfriend".

"She's here. Only wiser".

Upon reaching Jaiden's house, his house was packed with people, so we decided to take the back.

We are meaning the ones who had ketchup all over.

Jaiden was pissed as far as I could tell.

" Amber where have you been?" He asked looking at her and the state she was in.

"I'm sorry am late. I had something to do"

"Fine but guys can you please go clean up, you smell like when my dad is trying to cook".

He led us to his guest room apart from Amber who was in his room and allowed us to shower and change our clothes into the one's we brought.

I grabbed kataon's hand and head downstairs as I herd one of my songs playing.

Tonight we are young

I sang out loudly to the song by a guy named Fun who I loved his songs but not his name in the contrary.

We danced our night away and I enjoyed the first Halloween of my night, with actual persons I can call friends.

CHAPTER 29

"I hated Kat routine" Chelsey, one of the girls on the cheer team said.

"Every year its always the same foolish stuff. She did nothing knew only change its format".

I laughed as I heard them whine.

" What are you laughing at Mrs Miller? " One of them asked.

"I'm not married thank you" I said showing them my finger.

"I laugh because you guys only complaining but still didn't do anything. Right sis?".

But she didn't even take her eyes out of her phone.

" Shania?". I yelled.

"Huh yea sorry, you were saying".

" Travis isn't it?" I asked as she laughed.

"You know you guys are both lucky" Chelsey said.

"Lucky how" Hanna asked as she came into view with Amber and Johanna.

"We've been here for 6 years and couldn't even get Travis or Kataon to look at me and suddenly you guys came along and bomb, their yours"

Shania and I both laughed.

"I don't know but its anything but luck. Anyways I have an idea. Since the finals would be Friday, Shania and I could teach you guys an old routine we made but didn't do it because as you can see, we changed schools. We could show it to coach Parks".

They all agreed and soon, we set to work when the other girls left.

Kamera, your in for one hell of a fight.

" So how is this gonna work" I sat down beside Kevin who was now caught up in eating my moms cupcakes.

Sometimes I think that's the only reason why he comes here every night and not to see me.

"I don't know what is gonna happen but I know am gonna kick your mans butt on Friday night" Roger laughed.

It was so hard because I wanted to go with Kevin to cheer Roger on but how could I knowing that he'll be playing against my school.

"You mean my man's gonna kick your ass dude".

Kevin laughed.

" Did you just call my boyfriend dude" he said in between laughs.

I hit him on the shoulders. "Dude shut up".

Now Roger was laughing.

" What" I asked.

"Don't ever say the word dude again".

I rolled my eyes at the both of them.

" Thania sweet heart " my mom called from the kitchen.

"Be right back" I said getting up.

As I entered the kitchen, she pulls me into her small office like room.

"Dad won't be able to make it Friday, he has to work".

This was something normal.

"That's OK mom. If he doesn't work who else will pay for my new phone"

I laughed at her.

She kissed my forehead and I left.

As I went back to Kevin and Roger, Kevin looked pissed.

"What's the problem".

" Cupcakes" the only word that left Rogers mouth.

I laughed at the both of them.

"Sometimes I think he prefer the cupcakes over me".

Kevin and I both laughed at him as I rolled my eyes.

" Hell no" Kamera yelled as she shrieked at me.

"First you took my man,then you took my space at school then you took my squad. I hate you" she yelled at me.

The other girls and I was just finished showing coach Parks the routine we came up with.

"Kamera it is settled, we'll do something new for a change, I like this little routine of yours". She winked at me and turned towards the others.

"Catch this by tomorrow so we can finalize it by Thursday".

With nothing more she left.

Chelsey and the rest of us showed the girls the routine while Kamera and her two little bobble heads stood there watching.

Kamera stormed out of the auditorium as Brooke and Stephnee stood still until they both joined us.

" And our third-place winner is"

We all stood still as the announcer announced the top three winners for the finals.

"West Shore high school" I herd screams and cheers from the girls and boys who was on that team.

Looking around, our school was one out of two with boys not on the team.

I didn't care though, boys or no boys, we did great.

"Our second place winners are coming all the way from Isaac's all girls academy".

The same happened, cheers and applause.

That the was the girl schools to which Blake and Kevin attended.

Why did they have an a girls school and an all boys, why not mix it up.

"And our winner for this year's scholastic cheer finale is. Drum roll please".

My heart was beating so fast I swear I was hyperventilating.

" South Hampton high "

Oh my god we won. We won.

"We won. I can't believe we won"

We collected our trophy and took some pictures with the group.

Kamera even congratulated me on my routine, even coach Parks.

" Stop acting like a child " I said as I hit Kataon on the arm.

"We should have won, its my last year paying with my friends"

"I know but we can't have two winners"

"I know but I wanted another trophy".

Blake was now laughing at him as we all sat by the lake enjoying the rest of our night together as friends.

" So, you were saying" Roger said as he came up to me.

"You might have won the game tonight but I won also. And there was no way I was coming to the game in my cheer uniform and cheered for Isaac's all boys after we whopped the all girls butt".

Roger and I both laugh.

"Hey Roger. What's up with your schools. Why not one".

" Oh that. Si heard that Mr. and Mrs. Issac owned all school first and then they split so Mr. Issac build another school near ours and told Mrs. Issac that she could have the girls and he'll have the boys. Weird, I know".

"Hey guys, let's play a game". Haydn said breaking the silent.

" And that is? " Amber asked.

"Truth or sip" Jaiden said.

"No no" Belle said as we all looked at her.

"She's right. Remember what happened last time" Luke said

"Fine how about never have I ever. The skinny dip version".

" What" Shania and I asked at the same time.

They all laughed at us, even Roger and Kevin.

"You say something you've never done and if we did it, we take a piece of our clothes off, when your done to your last garment, you go skinny dipping"

We all agreed to play and so Amber started the game.

"Never have I ever had sex with with more than one guys".

Only Kevin and Roger removed a piece of garment causing all of us to laugh at them.

" My turn ". Travis said. "Never have I ever been skinny dipping"

This time only Johanna and Haydn remove something. We didn't even bother to question it.

"Ok. Now me" that was Belle.

"Never have I ever been to a strip club".

All the boys take something off, even Roger.

Kevin looked mad.

"Ok me". Now Luke.

"Never have I ever cheated in a relationship".

Now this was a surprise. No body took anything off.

We a looked around and started laughing.

" Now its my turn". Johanna said with a finger on her chin as if she was thinking then she spoke.

"Never have I ever have sexual fantasies about a teacher".

Only Kataon removed his under shirt.

So far I have everything on and Haydn had the least.

"My turn" I said causing everyone to look at me "

"Never have I ever had sex ".

And I was the only one who didn't take anything off.

" Bitch you're a virgin" Kevin asked laughing.

"Shut up". I shouted.

" Look game or not, I'm going swimming". Hanna stood up and took off what remaining clothes she had left and was left in her underwear and bra and ran in the water.

We all followed.

As soon as I was in the water, I felt two hands wrapped around me.

As I turned around, my lips met with his.

And I realize that this was gonna be the best year of my entire school life.

CHAPTER 30

"M om, where's my black boots?" I asked as I screamed down stairs to a busy mom.

Hearing no answer, I marched down to the kitchen.

"Oh hey honey". My dad had his tongue shoved down my moms throat.

" Gross ". A disgust Shania came down and yelled causing both my mom and I to laugh.

" You guys both know that that was what led to both of you right".

Shania and I both gaged causing us to laugh.

"Finish packing my dares?" My dad ask stealing one of mom's cupcakes earning him a swat on the hand.

"Yes about two nights ago" Shania replied with her head down in her phone.

"No because I can't find my boots".

"Oh I have them".

" Great " I replied to Shania. Note the sarcasm people. Just great.

"I'll go finish packing" I stated then headed upstairs just after my phone vibrated.

Kevin - Bitch I have a major crisis

Me - And that would be?

Kevin - Roger

Me - and Roger is a problem because?

Kevin - I won't be able to pick him up

Me - all you could have said was that I should pick Roger up * roll eyes*

Kevin - thanks bitch. I owe you and anyways how's that man cake of ours

Me - whatever and he's mine not ours and we are doing great maybe even better than expected.

Kevin - ok ttyl ily.

Pushing my phone into my pocket I made my way towards my room and got another text, but I decided to ignore until finishing packing.

Pushing Shania's room door, it was closed. Wait what. This was never closed before.

I pushed again and I heard her called out.

"I'm coming".

I waited for what felt like the longest minute of my life and then she finally opened the door.

" What took you so long?"

"I'm sorry I was just busy"

"Oh my god. He was here, wasn't he?"

She said nothing but held her head down.

"Eww" I jumped up from her bed that I was now sitting on seeing the sheets all ragged.

"Now my boots" I said reminding her of what I came for.

"Oh, yea here" she walked over to her closet and took my boots out.

Feeling my phone vibrating, I took it out.

Picking you up in 30 and tell Shania she's coming with us

Kataon:

Ok am finish packing and why can't Travis pick her up

Me:

Long story and pack a swim wearIt may be winter, but we have pools.

Kataon:

Ok. I love you

Me:

I love you too Kataon

Pushing my phone in to my pocket, I took my boots into my hand and watched as Shania changed her sheets.

Sitting down on her bed I told her what Kataon had told me and with it not being a surprise all she said was an ok.

"So where do you think mom and dad's going for their 20th anniversary celebration" I asked her as she put the last of her stuff in her suitcase.

"Bahamas" was Shania's answer.

"Oh my god. I so would kill to go there. Imagine a winter where you could still go to the beach and enjoy the warm sun"

"Well to bad it's an anniversary celebration and we're not invited".

Before I could answer her, I heard a car honking outside.

Knowing that it was Kataon, I ran downstairs.

" Hey babe "

"Hello to you too" my dad said causing my mom to laugh.

"Mr. and Mrs. Harris" Kataon said to my parents.

"Hello Kataon" my mom said as she turned towards Kataon.

"So where are you guys going for your anniversary?" He asked my mom.

"Bahamas" she replied with a huge smile.

"You seem enthusiasts"

"That's because I am. Now You guys should get going".

She waved us off as Shania and I left to what I want to be my best Christmas holiday ever.

Ok so I'm back home and as always, my mom wants to know everything so here I am giving her the details on what happened.

Christmas vacation is over.

I got to meet the twins which was so adorable.

My favorite memory was when Roger locked Shania and Amber outside after our round of Truth or Dare.

Kataon and I had a little conversation over who got to shower first since we are sharing the same room but not shower.

It was to say, a perfect Christmas.

"I would say I feel hurt, but I don't because I had a blast, and I can't wait to go back"

I told her about being asked officially to be girlfriend, how we celebrated Belle's birthday as apparently she was born the day after Christmas.

That was my mom rubbing her anniversary in my faces.

"To be honest your dad and I were abit scared when we just got hre and you didnt go as far as the door, always be in those books of uours"

It was fun, I never really pictured my senior year would have ended up like this, with genuine friends.

"I am proud of the young woman you are becoming Thania" she said to me as she took my hands into her.

"So what about me?" Shania asked coming from the kitchen, "I am proud of both of my girls" she said as Shania came and sit besdie mom causing both of us to sandwich her.

"You kno wif you told me this time last year that Thania would have had a boyfriend this time i definetaly would have laugh at that", Shania said looking at me laughing.

"Oh trust I would have laugh too" I said to her. "You guys do know I am sitting right here" my mom said to us causing both of us to laugh at her.

"I love you too Mom".

I kissed her on the cheek as I left her room with her giving me the goofy face.

EPILOGUE

"**5**,4,3,2,1"

"Happy new year"

We were at a new year Bonfire which was a yearly event here at South Hampton.

It wasn't so cold as it was in December and so even parents came out.

Unfortunately, my parents had to be at my mom's café because she was having a little new year togetherness according to her.

"So, a new year huh". Jaiden said.

"Yep" Shania replied popping the p.

"Wanna get out of here?" Travis asked

We all agreed leave.

About half an hour later, we arrived at the lake.

"So, who's going to take the first dip of the year? " Jaiden asks.

"I think the new additions to our group should go" Kataon replied giving me a kiss on the chin.

We've come a long way from where we've been when we just started dating.

His parents had dinner at my house on Christmas Eve and his little sister wouldn't let Shania out of sight.

As for Shania, Travis's parents and ours had a barbeque.

Trying to be the hard parent, my dad wanted to know the type of family that his daughter's boyfriend came from.

"Hey, can I ask a question? " I ask

"And that is " Blake said playing with Amber causing Johanna to laugh at them.

"How comes nobody but us ever comes out here? ".

"Oh, that's because it belongs to my parents ". Belle said.

"Ohk".

"So, what are we waiting for? " Shania asks.

Both Shania and I took our clothes off an was left in our bra an undies and ran right in, don't blame me I didn't pack a swimsuit, who knew I'd be swimming at 2 am in the morning.

As soon as Shania and I reached the water, the others started to join us and as always, we were on our respected pairs.

I couldn't have asked for a better new year.

Travis Hey, can you please tell Shania am outside waiting on her been calling her phone and no answer

Just as I hit the perfect sleeping spot here comes Travis waking me up via text.

"Shania" that was me yelling from my room to hers across the hall.

"What up sis?" She came barging in.

"Can you please go, your man is downstairs waiting for you and can you please tell him not whenever I'm asleep do not wake me up"

"Ok big sis" she said while rolling her eyes. " We are going bowling with a few of the guys, so I'll see you later"

She left and pulled the door up behind up behind her.

Just as I was about to go back to sleep here comes mom.

"Can you please come help me out at the shop the holiday got me going crazy"

Agreeing to her I got up and text Kataon about my plans an as I expected he said he'd be there to see me in the next half an hour.

Getting ready I threw a pair of leggings on with an oversized shirt I took from Kataons closet about some weeks ago. Mom and I head out and head over to the shop and just as she said it was chaos.

About 200 cupcakes later Kataon showed up with Joanna, Blake, Amber and Jaiden. And as I suspected the others were with Shania and Travis.

They stick around until my mom closed which was about 4 hours after. They played music, helped out mom and of course ate there ass off.

After that we all met up at Travis's house for the night since his parents were out of town.

"So how was your day babe?"

We were watching the movie Nine Ball, and it was dope, the boys wanted to watch it, but we told them if they did, we'd let all of us girls would sleep in the same room and as I thought we won.

Now here was Kataon trying to distract me from the movie.

"Babe?"

I'm not even going to pay him any mind.

None of us was paying any mind to the boys, about a minute later I saw them all left us by ourselves we all got closer to each other since they left.

And just like that, we were all wet.

Luke came out with a hose spraying all over of us. We started to scream and ran in different directions. Just know long story short, we were all soaked. Isabelle was now hitting like all over while water ran down on her.

We were all furious with the guys.

"I love you too babe" Luke said white kissing Belle on her forehead.

We all laughed at them.

"My homeboy here got an announcement to make y'all" Hayden yelled out.

"Isabelle" Luke spoke, "I know that this year isn't what you planned it to be but neither did I. I've always wanted something real, and I got that with you. Not only real but I got love, appreciation and everything that I ever ask for in a relationship"

I was speechless. He was now on his knees.

"I love you more than life itself. All I want to do is spend the rest of my life with you and be happy. I'm not asking you to give up your life and be with me just to accept that matter what I'll be there for you. Accept this ring as a sign of my love"

I was literally crying right now.

"Yes". Everyone was now looking the both of them kissing. He pulled away from the kiss talking again, "Marry me. You're the mother of...."

"Yes, a thousand times yes"

Issabelle said cutting off Luke.

We all clapped, hugged and congratulated both of them.

We all disappeared to our respective rooms looking forward to the future about to come for us as friends and soon family.

www.ingramcontent.com/pod-product-compliance
Lightning Source LLC
Chambersburg PA
CBHW071018180726
48291CB00004B/1518